The Translation of Enoch

The Translation of Enoch

Nick Harris

First published 2019 by

WORDS by DESIGN

www.wordsbydesign.co.uk

ISBN: 978-1-909075-80-1

Further copies of this book,
as well as details of other publications and services,
are available from

www.wordsbydesign.co.uk

Printed and bound by CPI Group (UK) Ltd, Croydon, CR0 4YY

With thanks to all who have helped this book be written
especially Freya and her boss.

1

'Don't let her catch you with your pants down' were the last words of instruction the sergeant had given. 'She'll want to come and climb up your...' The words of the fleshy-faced Sergeant Dromas were lost as the Landy pulled away, leaving Jonas to the desolation that was the Borderlands, South West Jordan CE2196.

Mercifully a cool breeze sprang up, a relief after the heat of the day. The dust danced and swirled, settling into every crease of Jonas's skin. It was inevitable that as the new boy he would get the short straw, not that the sergeant had anything against academy recruits he had assured him, 'just good to get some field experience under your belt... also up your nose, in your eyes behind your ears' Jonas was in the Borderlands; a barren heartless environment, a haven for those who would harm the Citadel.

He could still conjure up the grins on the faces of his fellow dragoons as the sergeant outlined the day's activity. Scouting ahead of the air conditioned patrol vehicle, Jonas was to look for signs of life. If he came across anything unusual he was to call it in. His hover jet's range was up to three miles from the main group going east to west, the Landy patrolling the northern sweep.

Normally such duties were split into shorter shifts but, as the sergeant said with mock seriousness, it would be good for Jonas to have an extended first date with the 'bitch' – his name for the area.

It had proved to be a long day that followed with nothing to report. The 'bitch' had been quiet. Now Jonas ached in places he hadn't known existed, his head swam with tiredness from the glare of sun-baked sand, and he was ready for the shift to end.

Steering toward towering peaks of the eastern ridge, Jonas was preparing to make a final turn when movement in the distance flickered past his peripheral vision.

He was turning to head back to the main group when he saw it again: movement on the edge of a valley now in shadow as the sun set. Jonas made a cautious approach then he abruptly halted the machine, surprise widening his eyes as out of the shadow stepped an embodiment of the bitch herself not more than 30 feet ahead.

Here was the very personification of arid beauty. She stood before him, coal black eyes, wind-sculpted features, breasts accentuated by flowing yet clinging robes that revealed and then hid long dark limbs, a perfect form crowned with a mass of restless hair. The beauty was utterly present to Jonas's eye for what seemed like forever. And he drank her in. Breaking the spell with a mesmerizing grace, the bitch moved, her arms extended enticing Jonas towards her, and then she was engulfed once more by shadow.

Jonas became aware of a thunderous shaking of the ground to his left where, mounted on a fierce horse, its teeth bared, ears flat back against a massive skull, the apparition of a moment ago took a very real form appearing grim-faced, eyes blazing, hair flying, with a drawn sabre. Flashing hooves bore down on the frozen trooper.

It was only instinct that saved Jonas; he ducked the scything blade that was carried away by the momentum of the charge. With an exhilaration that overwhelmed his fears and the sergeant's command, Jonas turned his machine and set off in pursuit. Ahead lay his prize, at full gallop lying virtually flat along the back of the dun coloured horse, it was no match for a hover jet, this bitch wasn't getting away. Jonas's desire to catch and kill was fuelled by the knowledge that this was the fast-track way out of a harsh posting. He had no desire to be one of the few of the dragoons in the Citadel stuck in this forsaken hellhole for years on end. Jonas saw the rider slow fractionally preparing to leap a fissure; a sharp turn in the wadi-bed lay yet further ahead before the steepening climb into the encircling hills.

Urging the machine on, Jonas pressed ahead. Despite the helmet filters he could taste the dust from the racing hooves and it was the sweet taste of victory; the kill was close. Jonas activated the rifle in readiness for the triumphant conclusion as the rider reached the turn in the track and with graceful fluidity turned sharply out of sight.

Slowing to make a more cumbersome turn, Jonas was around the corner seconds later, now full power in a straight-line charge would bring him within unmissable range. He sped up the valley to the visibly tiring rider. Drawing the now armed rifle he prepared to bring down his quarry, allowing himself a sense of triumph, because for Jonas, dragoon of the 2nd squad of the border patrol, today would be the day when everything changed.

Virtually invisible to the naked eye, it was the tautly stretched wire that changed everything. Seconds earlier it had lain inert on the floor as flying hooves pounded over it. Now immense power raised it to life, a vibrating tension held at neck height anticipating the onrushing trooper. Jonas's head was flying through the air. Eyes wide open, brain still processing, Jonas saw the rider wheel and charge to meet him in some macabre embrace, arms outstretched to catch his flying head, deftly snatching it from the air. With his life light fading, Jonas beheld his rifle and his hover jet before fading to darkness.

'Quickly! Get them here.' The now dismounted figure snapped out orders to a small group emerging from the site of ambush. The rider ripped the visor from the dying dragoon, and grabbing the proffered rifle activated the iris recognition security that returned the weapon to its default 'in arsenal' state available for use. The hover jet stubbornly refused to unlock and with a resigned sigh, dragoon Jonas's head was flung into the scrub, his now lifeless eyes unable to unlock the machine to be used by others.

'This isn't getting any easier, Zenobia; you run greater risks for what, a rifle? How will one rifle rid of us of these aggressors?' Turning with a sigh, the rider stood and stretched her aching spine arching upwards whilst reaching towards the reddening sky. Her dark eyes were set within a flawless olive skin topped with a tangle of ringlet curls. Zenobia smiled with a stunning innocence of one who rejoiced in death.

'One by one if needs be, Spiro, one more for us, one less for them. That was good work on the wire today, this dragoon "Jonas" was getting quite close to taking me, thank you.'

As always she touched his heart with her words and her conviction. As with all her ragtag army the massive Spiro followed the dream that was Zenobia, a dream that one day freedom would be tasted, livings could be established in good lands free from violence and oppression. For years the aggression against Spiro's kith and kin had built, forcing them to the very margins of existence on the Great Heights, fearful of returning to what was once their home in the Borderlands.

They had been mercilessly driven from these lands by the Citadel, demoralised and leaderless until this warrior princess had arisen phoenix-like from the ashes of her bereavement, determined to destroy Abbadon.

'We must hurry, Spiro, before his friends come looking for their comrade. Let's get this corpse set up.' With cheerful indifference to the visceral vestige of the day's work the two set about dragging first corpse, then hover jet and finally the head towards the base of the cliff wall that formed the opening to the narrowing ravine.

Already the censors on both rifle and machine would be signalling in distress the location to the main patrol, which would hopefully lead them ‘headlong’ as Zenobia liked to quip, into sharing something of a similar fate.

Before long the sound of approaching dragoons was thrumming ominously in the air. Soon they too would become a votive offering to be laid on the ancient altar that was the grave of Zenobia’s family.

2

A diffused light cast mote-filled illumination into the library. Haphazardly stacked volumes were touched by its rays, their golden lettering reflecting the hazy light. The young man continued turning papers, their movement slowly adding to the occluded atmosphere. The books were as yet untouched by his enquiring hands for he sought words in the loose sheaves of paper. From time to time the pronunciation of a word intrigued him sufficiently that he would try it out. Rolling a word around his tongue like a fine wine before spitting it out – 'Sodomite'

'Bless you!' came a reply from within the depths of a wing-backed chair.

'Pardon?' Young enquiring eyes met hazel brown orbs that contained a hint of amusement as well as challenge in a face as leathery as his chair.

'I said, "bless you". You've found an arcane phrase, and I've matched it with another.' Amused, Hanok waited, observing the processing of thought in the young man.

'Bless you; may God bless you. When your word "sodomite" punctured the silence it was like a sneeze. In ages past it was feared you could sneeze out your soul and "bless you" or "may God bless you" was a ward against such a fate.'

'That's a lot of words in response to one. What do they mean –

"soul", "God" and "Bless" and for that matter "sodomite"?'

It was proving to be another trying day for Dan. Eyes aching from prolonged focus on ancient script, the pupil again chided himself. Not for the first time doubt rose within him; why was he here? A few weeks before life had been very different for Dan; he was considered a fine scholar, achieving results that were the top of an elite cadre. With a sharp mind, a strong physique, and a winning personality Dan had become a very attractive young man. Taller than his contemporaries, he had blond hair that remained sufficiently controlled to frame the strong jaw and slightly aquiline nose. With a fair complexion, easy smile, and feline grace, Dan was someone who was winning at life. The Telemeric Corporation, pleased to see the results of their selection programme, were quick to offer an internship at the heart of the organisation. When the opportunity to assist one of the finest minds in the Corporation was brought to his attention, he grasped at what the fates had offered. Now that opportunity had sadly lost its allure. He felt a kinship with the faded guilt lettering on the spines of the works that now surrounded him. Life for the young aspiring graduate of medicine was not entirely happy.

As he observed the student's demeanour, light faded slightly from the older man's gaze as he answered his question. 'Dan, we have these words, a rare collection of words, yet we know little of their meaning. There was once a time, perhaps hundreds of years past, when these words and others carried power. You might use a word such as "sodomite" in a way that damaged, forever, the life of another. Terrible consequences followed such a word, if you were branded a sodomite... Men lost their jobs, faced prison, harsh corrective chemical treatment, even death. All because of a word, a badge of shame tying a person to a city long gone where lust, not love, was violently expressed. Now these words are lost to our world and that's a good thing for some words... but to know, Dan, to know the meaning of words – the ideas, hopes and dreams that they convey, is an adventure, a treasure to seek. A quest, Dan, seeking that which is lost, so much so that if we find it then…' The light faded again and the animated features returned to their resting composure.

Sadness settled on Hanok as energy departed the study and stillness re-joined the couple. The stillness was disturbed as Hanok eased his frame in the chair. 'Dan, ever since we lost the meaning of words now considered defunct, we have lost meaning in our life. Or that's how it seems to me, and some others. We have pushed so hard for the future that the past has been lost to us, and the past may contain the answers we need. Here in this room is the past, the embodied ancient wisdom of the world, or what we have left of it. We are all products of our past to some extent, Dan, you included. I wonder if you realise quite what it is that lies within you.'

Dan sighed as he looked around the room, lost in thought. *If the high and heavy shelving are anything to go by in this musty place, whatever is within me it is buried mightily deep.* He had witnessed Hanok's descent into despondency, maybe two or three times during his time with him, usually when they were seated as now in the library. It was as if the futility of the work, the sheer scale of the task, broke over him as a wave drenching him in despair.

The library had grown incrementally as Hanok sought secrets and wisdom from the past in search of answers to dangers that he feared would overwhelm the life of the Citadel itself. Following the fiery destruction of most books in a terrible accident, the writings that Hanok had gathered had become a priceless treasure to be held in this one place of safety. For years Hanok had dedicated his life to seeking that which was lost. Dan sighed — *really, ancient wisdom? more like decrepit ramblings;* all Dan seemed to have were lists of words, and how these might help the aged man was lost to him. Tiredness added an edge to his voice.

'But they're just words,' he said, 'random words. Some have context but most on this sheet stand in splendid isolation. How can I make sense of a word like "Sodomite" without your explanation? How can this be considered an adventure, where are the new discoveries? What is the point of all this drudgery other than an old man's fantasy?' The words tumbled out as an assault and accusation that was unintentionally hurtful, an outburst of weary frustration.

It seemed to Dan that he'd taken a first wrong step in life, and the loss of his surefooted confidence had occurred just as he took his very first step onto the corporate ladder. Frustration gave rise to a spiteful tone and wounding tongue; instead of the bright future dreamed of, he was stuck in the reality of a dreary task. Whatever the reasons for them, words once spoken could not be taken back, a shame for Dan as they evoked a response that exploded into the room.

'Yes I know they're just words!' Hanok rose fiercely from the chair. 'Lost and broken from context, they have little currency for someone like you!' Spittle flecked the dried lips and flew as arrows towards the young man. 'But for me, I know, I believe that there are some words, perhaps hidden in plain sight, that contain life and hope. I am sick of a life that is endless; no medication satisfies this longing for another way. It has grown in me like one of those once feared cancers. I refuse to believe there is no more to life than this, this... sensory management and somatic maintenance that we now call living.'

Towering in passion Hanok began moving around the room, plucking at paper-bound manuscripts, individual sheets waving in procession as he passed by in his wrath. 'Dan, I have read of something wonderful, so wonderful that I have to encounter it, experience it and enter into it for myself. I have heard of a life that is not endless but that is *eternal*, rich and beautiful. It calls to me when I dream, whispers in the shadows of my heart. Somehow we have lost sight of such a life, lost access to it when we discarded our books those ages ago. Yet now I feel them, Dan; out there calling to us are words that we consider unimportant. To hear them speak as we read them again, Dan, that could change everything.' The fierce intensity of the Elder's progress subsided, the papers stilled in anticipation of what was to be said next. Dan, stunned by the outburst, held very still. 'I have read words that hold a key, that could unlock that life... it is in this place, part of a collection of writings. But where? Returning after journeying in some desolate places has injured my mind, my memory seems to fail me and frailty catches up like a pursuing hound. It's extraordinary, that just on the verge of discovery of life I am finally facing death, endless life is a myth, we have built a Citadel on a lie.' A deep sadness welled in the brown eyes that considered the pupil. 'I don't quite know why, Dan, but I asked specifically for you to help me these past weeks because I sense you could reveal that which I cannot grasp. You must find these words because they hold a clue to life that is hidden. I fear it will be a hard task, dangerous and mysterious, for there are forces at work that would see its secrets buried for good – or should I say for evil.'

Sitting heavily, the Elder closed his eyes, his head hung forward and he sighed deeply into sleep. *Silly sod,* thought Dan, then a breath, sweetly scented, passed over him. 'I wonder what that means?' he said to the room in general.

3

The brightly lit complex of the Citadel floated high over barren land; a perfect cube, it extended many miles in every direction gently vibrating, and it was held in acoustic tension by troughs of returning sound waves produced within the complex that resonated, returning amplified from the Borderlands, untroubled by its tremors. A triumph of human ingenuity constructed with virtually indestructible glass and super-tensioned polycarbonate, the Citadel was a secure home for the elect people who were recognised in international law as a nation state replete with foreign embassies. It was not as yet self-sufficient in every regard and maintained access to the ground via moveable portals enabling political, military and trading links to be maintained with the world outside. Within the vastness, discreet screens had been activated; the chosen colour for the week of violet provided the required privacy and solemnity for a meeting of the board of the Telemeric Corporation, who were now two hours into their third session. Twenty-four of the wisest heads were gathered, seated in a circle to hear from Hanok who dominated the centre of the room. His message was grim, the atmosphere was taut, a mixture of disbelief and distress.

'We have a problem the like of which has not troubled us before. It is an increasingly complex situation that, left unresolved, threatens our existence!'

Standing amongst the Convocation of seniors, Hanok sought to put his case, one that would be listened to in a respectful silence, for this presentation was the fruit of the many months of labour of a well-respected, if somewhat eccentric, mind.

'Without acknowledging the problem, how can we even begin to seek a solution? What shall be said of us in times to come if we do nothing? Increasingly our predictors tell us that there will be a failure in Telomerase management, we can't be confident that ageing can be held back. We claim to have defeated death itself; we tell our people we've modified their Telomeres, re-capped the DNA strands to prevent their shortening, ageing is a thing of the past, as their DNA is endlessly repairable. We manage perfectly the biochemical and physiological process of each human, rectifying the homeostatic imbalances. We live endlessly; it is a triumph!'

Gathering himself, Hanok dropped his voice to a whisper, drawing the assembled seniors of the Telemeric Corporation towards his conclusion.

'Yet in our triumph lies our tragedy. We've failed to see that endless life is actually finite. Cases of degeneration are reported that we cannot halt. A very gradual degeneration, granted, but a sign of things to come – and come with increasing swiftness... people in our care are dying.' Hanok drew back his shoulders and raised his head in defiance. He knew such talk would be regarded as heterodox nonsense yet the evidence was clear to him. Humans were failing to respond to *Telemoriese*, the medication that halted ageing, allowing the nearly forgotten signs to edge onto the margins of the human form, memory function seemingly the first to be afflicted, followed by loosening skin tone and muscle wastage.

He recalled even now his dismay when he visited the homes of those who were slipping into old age. Sanitised cells where confused and frightened faces held the expression of sadness lost to all in another world. Hanok had travelled widely in his research, something that was quite rare as the need to travel for leisure, study or commerce was largely redundant, virtual reality being the only reality people required. Travel had opened Hanok's eyes to a world that was far less sanitised than he imagined. As a senior leader he had access to areas otherwise prohibited and had seen life in the raw. Most of the people he encountered were content with an existence that was freed from the mundane and chemically enhanced. But every now and then, almost from the corner of his eye, another story presented itself to Hanok; one that was fully told when he stumbled by chance across the homes.

With a polite cough another rose to speak, '*If* the conclusions of our much respected wise friend of the Corporation are correct, we would indeed face very uncertain times.' The smooth base tones dripping with natural authority washed over the Convocation. 'Of course, '*if*' is the point, we don't know this is happening. A few minor mutations can't be the basis of panic. *If* such news of failure of life leaked from here to the people, consternation would descend into chaos, how could we continue as a race? Let's not forget how long it has been since the last wet birth occasioned by fluid exchange!'

Most, but not all, chuckled at the reference to the now archaic notion of chance being allowed to play a part in producing new humans. 'Fluid exchange' was the mocking term for human reproduction that occurred away from the test tubes. These days so few new human beings were required for an overcrowded Citadel of endless lives, that only a carefully selected few came about. It was a sensible management of resource; synths did the work of the 'young' so well that uncontrolled production of more people was widely regarded as selfish and wasteful.

'*If*,' the honeyed voice continued, '*If* this problem were real, could you imagine the panic? We're almost incapable of reproducing our race. We love our medication and the transcendence it brings. We contain the risk of entry into life with specialist incubators; how would we replicate anywhere near enough new humans to sustain ourselves if we began to see death amongst us? All we have gained would be thrown to those dogs up on the heights. My friends, all the evidence we see is that our medication is effectively managing bios. That is the message that must come from Telemeric. Any talk of failure and fault is fanciful farce.' Drawing threateningly close to the now seated Hanok, the speaker's voice gained a hard edge. 'Elder Hanok has our thanks for containing his concerns within the Convocation; he must not repeat them outside our number, I hope that is clear.'

Gazing slowly around the gathered faces, most of whom had served the corporation from its virile growth to its triumph as the dominate and ultimately only multi-national corporation that operated in the Citadel, dominating its people, the honey-toned Marcus smiled to see that again they agreed with him. Secure in his authority, he decided it was time to extend the conciliatory hand. '*If*, on the other hand there are these... oddities of information abroad, we must look into them discreetly. Our science can provide answers to the irregularities, of that I have no doubt.' Smiling, he continued, 'and *if* Elder Hanok wished to explore any other implications of his prognosis for our *condition*, we should encourage him to share his findings with us who will, of course, give him our support and blessing and again our thanks for his courageous discourse today.'

Sometime later, seated alone after the conclusion of the meeting, Marcus Dromas, Senior Director of the Telemeric Corporation and leader of the Citadel's governing council, brooded darkly over the recent events in his opulent office at the heart of the citadel.

There were slight fissures of doubt that rose from his gut to his mind, and albeit subtle they touched a part of Marcus long dormant.

Dismissing the possibility of the truth in Hanok's speech, Marcus focused on managing information. Everyone must stay on message, everyone must believe, this heresy of fragility could not be tolerated – the only truth acceptable would be controlled by the corporation. As he brooded, a heavy presence rose up as a comforting mist and seemingly settled upon his frame, affirming in whispered words the rightness of Marcus's darkening thoughts.

~ ~ ~

Events of the Convocation, now long passed, looped in Hanok's mind. He slept surrounded by the comforting papers of the library. He had been given their blessing to seek out evidence of his fears, but what he was searching for went far beyond that. What he had witnessed was a horror. Confused and despairing eyes of the elderly, their piteous cries for help gripped him reaffirming the rightness of the quest. Voices whispered and called him forward, encouraging the search for truth with a sweet sublime urgency hidden from his waking mind.

Other voices of a deeper and more menacing tone arose from hidden depths that intensified the fear in those aged ones, a desolation that claimed their very existence. Hanok's long gaunt frame trembled, bearded lips moving in a silent cry as he battled against the call of the darkness, resisting with all his strength its lure towards oblivion. Such were the forces set loose in Hanok that enduring and restful sleep was rarely experienced.

He opened his eyes to discover he was alone; Dan had disappeared. The only door from the room remained bolted from within. Dan's pile of papers lay scattered nearby; the first of the bound volumes that he was due to examine lay brutalised before him with many pages wrenched from their fastening. Instinctively he knew that a coldness had entered the sanctuary of the library, and the hairs rose on Hanok's arms, a response not to the fall in temperature but the presence of evil.

4

The practice of the Borderland force was to patrol in heavily fortified troop Land Patrol Vehicles capable of carrying a dozen dragoons, as well as a driver and commander. These vehicles were supplemented by hover jets that acted as forward scouts and were supported by drones capable of providing air support should overwhelming force be encountered. Armed with rocket launchers, cannon and laser, 'Landies' were the beloved work horse of the patrol, far superior to anything ever encountered 'out there'.

Landy 93 nosed its way cautiously into the ravine mouth, rounding the 90 degree entrance, and edged forward. Sergeant Dromas, peering out through the forward observatory, thought he glimpsed Jonas. Clearly something was amiss; the hover jet lay at a near perpendicular angle seemingly embedded in rock with Jonas trapped between machine and cliff. The scanners gave no sign of life.

This was a recovery job, corpse and machine back to base to analyse the flight data recorders. The accepted procedure for recovery was to reverse up to the crash site, the armaments reassuringly forward facing to deter whatever might be lurking in the area whilst the cliff face protected the rear.

Dromas was keen to get on with the work and get out of this doleful place that carried a weight of foreboding the superstitious sergeant liked not one bit. His unease fed back to the squad, all of whom knew that but for the duty roster it could so easily be their corpse that was now becoming flyblown and bloated. Sergeant Dromas knew that he would have to answer for the death of a trooper from the Citadel on his first tour. It was one thing to lose a mercenary, quite another to lose one of your own. The sergeant regretted his beasting of the boy, a venting of his frustration at the endless years he had patrolled this forsaken wilderness.

With swift deft manoeuvres the Landy was aligned ready for the final reverse, despite the sergeant's preoccupation with the trouble he was in. Shadows deepened as light fled from depths of the valley, the setting sun impotent. Dromas tried to shake off the eerie sense that the shadows of the valley of death were extending eager fingers towards the patrol vehicle; he shuddered again to shed the thought and sent the vehicle further back.

From her vantage point Zenobia impassively observed the encroaching vehicle. With good fortune, the pits dug overnight and now camouflaged would remain undetected until the machine had fallen. As she signalled to those on her left and right, the levering poles were rammed into the bases of boulders, with ten people on each taking the strain, the rocks beginning to shift as the poles groaned threatening to shatter and impale the attackers as they sharded. Back came the vehicle closer and closer as the strain of wood and flesh intensified to a crescendo, until with a groaning the massive slab of sandstone began to move.

Dromas rechecked the scanners for hostile persons, and finding none gave the order to recover the fallen whilst accelerating the machine the final 30 feet towards the rock face. As the heavy door was swung open and the recovery team readied themselves to exit the vehicle with body bags and winches, the offside rear-drive wheels found the deep traps. The Landy lurched downwards dropping into the six-foot grave, men tumbling.

Furiously switching the direction of travel, Dromas engaged forward drive and began to crawl the Landy out of the trap. The noise was terrifying as the engine screamed, gears tortuously grinding metal on metal as Dromas sought to get the machine moving. Fear gripped Dromas as the rumble of a rock fall intensified and figures were emerged wraith-like in the dust, impassive, waiting, vengeful. One advanced holding a severed head he ran at Dromas, throwing the bloody mess against the screen where for a moment the lifeless eyes looked deeply into Dromas's own, calling him towards his doom. The wheels fought for grip and began to gain forward momentum, the screams from the pit were clearly audible to him as the bodies of the fallen troopers became means of traction, the wheels biting in, driving forward mercilessly.

Just as it seemed the Landy would shake itself free the larger rocks fell smashing all hope of escape, the interior of the transport was peeled open, and the visceral stench filled the nostrils of Dromas. He was pinned within the crushed metal of the Landy, with the stench of broken bodies and leaking fuel making his senses swim. Dromas remained alive, his chest numb, rock-pierced, his head swimming and blood ebbing from his broken form a reddening pool growing larger at his feet, the smell of his loosened bowels still fetid in his nostrils, a memory of many deaths he had witnessed. The sergeant looked into the same coal black eyes of the 'bitch'. Somewhere in their depths lay a sadness that death was coming to claim Sergeant Dromas, who closed his eyes to the inevitable.

5

'Gone! How can they be gone?' Frumentus stared wide eyed at Marcus whose features were alive with triumph; writhing serpent-like lips hissed out a reply. 'Yes gone, you fool, lost forever. Frumentus the Fool has deleted the legacy of humanity in a single act of folly.' Contemptuous eyes burned deeply into the young man, hot breath searing his fleshy face, a physical menace forcing Frumentus to back further against the sharp and piercing edge of the control panel that hummed with animosity in the brightly lit room.

All had started so well. Frumentus, the newly installed Head of Security of the Citadel, had been delighted that importance had finally come his way. No longer would he drag around the crippling disapproval of his forebears, for at last he had achieved a position of significance. Many had smiled at his naivety, not necessarily unkindly for one who didn't quite fit into the way things were. Head of Security in a place where no crime occurred, aged in appearance where signs of ageing were banished, persistent in duties that were more ceremonial than serious, a court jester. People needed a Frumentus, someone to be the measure by which false bearings could be taken and mistaken inferences drawn.

'Yes gone, lost forever. Fool! What possessed you? Why did you incinerate forever the writings of the wise; are you so contemptuous of the past? Here in the heart of the Citadel, which should be the place of safety, where we've painstakingly gathered the wisdom of the ages entombed in deep vaults secure from air and sunlight, insect and spores. "Saved for the future, available to the present, drawn from the past," that was our promise now incinerated in seconds by your actions.'

Ashamed, Frumentus withdrew, turtle-like, from Marcus's wrath. Frumentus the Fool who burned the wisdom of the world by mistake. It was a doomsday exercise to test readiness, nothing serious or out of routine of Citadel life. Just a drill, a dummy run now, he stood as mute as a mannequin, wordlessness his only defence. He'd followed procedure: category A intrusion, final security breached, the destruction of the Citadel's secrets a priority. At the penultimate incineration he'd requested the final code, randomly selected and advised from outside the complex, and entered it. Even now the furious heat erupting from the chamber like some vast bellow of a mythical beast could be felt on Frumentus's crestfallen face – gone, every manuscript, all hard drives, everything cataclysmically consumed.

The word echoed in Frumentus's mind as he surveyed the scene before him, books and papers giving mute testimony to his failure. The face of Hanok gazing in puzzlement at him; 'gone, that's right gone, disappeared from my locked rooms with violence done to a manuscript and maybe to my man. Do you see? Are you listening to me? Are you alright?'

Gathering himself, Frumentus tried to focus on the present. In the heart of the Citadel it appeared that a crime had occurred. Property was missing and by all accounts a promising young student had vanished. The room itself – Frumentus decided 'crime scene' would be the right description – the crime scene was a puzzle. Firstly it was occupied by Hanok alone, though signs of another presence were clearly evident. Secondly it contained the undamaged remains of writings that Hanok had gathered from the central store to form his own private library, apparently assuring the custodians that these were necessary for his research. Thirdly, linked to the second point, absolutely no technology was allowed anywhere near what was left. No security monitoring, no electromagnetic locks, no external overrides that might fall into the hands of – well someone like Frumentus. The old man had awoken to a scene of crime, his assistant and a book absent, the bolt operated vertically over the top of the door firmly and snugly shot downwards in a locked position. The windows were set high in the walls, non-opening and unbroken. The floor appeared solid as did the walls, although they were book-lined so perhaps a way out lay behind them.

Straitening his rather crumpled uniform, Frumentus set to work.

'Check for points of egress, biological traces and signs of struggle, please, Shylock.' Shylock, the security synth, appeared to sigh before casting a scanning eye around the room. Quite how Frumentus had been allocated a synth with attitude was beyond his comprehension. It was very useful to have a mobile crime laboratory available to him as Head of Security, an asset in daily matters of security extensively linked to the networks, able at a moment's notice to provide valuable intelligence. But why did it have to be grumpy?

Sometimes, in his weaker moments, Frumentus felt Shylock was present more in a restraining capacity. He hadn't lost his job following the book burning, he'd gained a synth and one that seemed highly capable of ensuring security was never compromised; buttons were never erroneously pressed and Frumentus never exceeded the budget.

'There is one door, the windows are entire, there are no hidden exits, security is primitive – sir.' There it was again, a slightly delayed, reluctantly given acknowledgement of authority. Frumentus frowned – perhaps he was just too sensitive. Removing his cap, he ran his hand over a stubbly head before rubbing the fleshy back of his neck, seeking both inspiration and calm whilst deep in thought.

How then was it possible for Dan to disappear through a door bolted from the inside, could this Hanok have had a hand in his disappearance? Why would he possibly want to engineer that? How could a synth manage to look smug...?

Sighing inwardly, Frumentus returned his gaze towards the greatly respected man. 'Can you help me understand why the young man and the manuscript might have been taken from here?

Hanok lifted a perplexed hand. 'I'm also at a loss to know who, how or why this happened, perhaps what has gone is significant to my research – but sadly I don't know what is was. Dan was working his way through all these papers.'

Moving to the defiled documents, Hanok pondered the mystery of the missing manuscript. 'It seems in part to be a report on the visit of James Bruce, Freemason and seeker of mysteries, to Ethiopia the land of Cush, circa 1800. He had discovered something amidst the ancient libraries known as Genizots, ancient burial sites for books, scraps of writing and other bits and pieces. Whatever it was excited his interest sufficiently to expend considerable sums in collecting and translating what transpired to be apocryphal writings, *The Book of Enoch.* By all accounts of little interest to the wider world of his day.'

Frumentus puzzled at the crime scene. He knew that a young man who had clearance to work here had vanished along with one book, appearing on no movement sensors outside the room. The alarm was raised 48 hours ago. No sightings had been reported nor detectors triggered throughout the complex. Frumentus noted that there was a radius of several feet away from the door before these sensors became operational. Might Dan have stumbled across something sinister? How could you disappear through a solid bolted door? Gloomily Frumentus stared at the floor; a book burning and a burglary: not a great record for Head of Security, would his next posting be to the Borderlands? No one chose those wilderness places to spend their days.

The faintest sound of a cough caught his ear, and looking up Frumentus found Shylock looking down at the floor by the solidly bolted door. 'May I suggest how the young man and the writing disappeared through the door – sir?' There it was again, that pause. Frumentus wasn't given to violence but today something snapped within the Head of Security, a thing so tightly wound by the sly smiles and outright mockery that was his daily lot, that it caused considerable momentum and extensive force to swing through his right leg planting a firm foot in the backside of the synth accompanied by a curse.

Pain was not a sensation that synths were programmed to display, surprise was allowed for and puzzlement thought a useful way of empathetic bonding. Shylock did his best to stick to these responses following Frumentus's wild attack, whilst storing away the darker energies released by the fool.

Outright belly laughing was not a response expected from a synth and indeed it was the older man who was gripping his sides, bent nearly double at the sight of Frumentus painfully holding his foot whilst hopping around the floor. Synths had reinforced rears housing their power packs, a fact Frumentus seemed to have forgotten, and Hanok's laughter served as a voluble reminder to Frumentus the Fool.

~ ~ ~

Deep in the bowels of the earth, in a darkened room away from prying eyes, Dan emerged from his own darkness to find himself bound and looking at a screen flickering with images of the naked female form.

‘Do you see them?’ asked a crystal voice near Dan’s ear, cold lips seemingly brushing his lobe. ‘Look. Are they not wondrous? We watch them, we see them, we know them, we desire them. Open your eyes, look, are they not… gorgeous. Are you not engorged?’

Dan struggled to focus on anything, heaviness seemingly settled into his bones as blood thundered through his veins. The voice when it came again pierced all, reaching into the very core of being. ‘What beauty of shape, what soft curving delicate forms, what lustrous hair. Oh, how we lust for them; for we see them! Do you not see, will you not look? Come, my fine young man, behold the wonder of creation drawn out from your side. Behold flesh of your flesh, bone of your bone.’

Something gripped the blond mane and jerked it harshly upwards, as a heavy slap shocked some clarity into Dan. Swaying, tired and confused, Dan tried to look, tried to see. ‘No,’ he croaked, throat raw and burning voice faint. ‘I can’t see.’

The crystal voice, breath sweetly scented, withdrew into the gloom with a whispering sigh. The scented breath reached into the depth of Dan’s consciousness. Dan was utterly lost to exhaustion and enfolded in darkness. He sank yet deeper into despair, tears flowed silently into the darkness.

6

'I am sorry, Frumentus I didn't mean to laugh, how is your foot?'

Looking up from the leather chair, until recently the resting place for the older man, Frumentus was slightly overwhelmed by the genuine concern and compassion emanating from Hanok.

'I'm also sorry for my outburst, I know it's ridiculous but there's something sly about Shylock. Yes, I know he's a synth and devoid of slyness but, well, he's almost rude sometimes.' Embarrassed at his actions and now that he'd named an unspoken fear, Frumentus felt a different warmth creep up his neck onto his face.

'My dear man, don't be embarrassed, I'll not say a word about this. I have something that might help your foot, which does seem rather swollen, and as far as I can tell no harm has come to Shylock.' The aforementioned stood by the door gazing impassively towards the humans, neither dented nor diminished by recent events.

Before long life was looking a good deal better for Frumentus, and he was enjoying Hanok's conversation. The ageing man seemed to have a genuine interest in Frumentus's life and struggles. It was as if a burden was being lifted as Hanok listened to him intently, gradually elements of his life and failures coming to the surface only to be met with a gentle smile or word of encouragement.

Frumentus bathed in the unconditional positive regard of another human being as he talked on and on whilst his foot was treated. So relaxed was he that the story of the book burning was relayed without thought, and it was only the tightened grip on his foot that caused Frumentus to stop speaking and focus on the face of Hanok, a face that itself had gone a very dark colour indeed.

'Marcus? The Director of the Corporation and Citadel, that Marcus! He was with you when the fire came!?' Eyes blazing, Hanok was intensely focused away in the mid distance as if seeing something for the first time. 'He was there instigating the destruction.'

'No, it was my fault, I pressed the button, I entered the code. It was my fault, my shame, I am to blame. I am sorry, no one was to know this, it was to be our secret and now I have failed again! What a fool am I!' Tears flowed freely, the secret he was to keep had been let loose.

Poor Frumentus crumbled. 'Please, I can't betray his trust. He was so angry when I got the whole exercise wrong and destroyed the writings. Saved for the future, available to the present, drawn from the past, destroyed by a fool.' Misery once again engulfed Frumentus.

Marcus had allowed him to keep his position and decided he wouldn't release the cause of the destruction to safeguard the good name of Frumentus's family, longstanding and close friends of the Corporation as they were. In return Frumentus was to say nothing and admit to nothing concerning those fateful events. But with Hanok he felt able to unburden.

'I got the override code wrong, reversing just two digits in the sequence was all it took.' Frumentus could feel the heat of shame as fiercely upon him as the jets of flame that filled and consumed the immense chamber.

'The code sequence, who gave you that?'

Eyes bright with interest, Hanok listened in wonderment. Could such things be true, that such a simple error could lead to the destruction of the written wisdom, and could Marcus have relayed the error? Pushing such thoughts to the back of his mind, he turned to the undented synth.

'So, Shylock, to return to your discovery, how did Dan disappear through a solid door that is internally bolted?'

7

Some things are deeply buried for their protection; others are entombed for the protection of others. Marcus couldn't decide which it was for the external control room. He had been summoned by the Controllers and his unease was accentuated as he entered the darkened subterranean chambers that lay outside the Citadel. He shuddered inwardly; in this place he could not escape the sense that he was known, and deep within his survival instinct sounded an alarm bell.

He took a grip of himself and pushed further into the gloom; he was Marcus Dromas, the Director, there was nobody in the Corporation that he feared but here, away from the Citadel, Marcus felt exposed. He knew the powerful patronage that the Controllers provided but they were mysterious, this would be his first face to face.

Marcus drew himself up to his full height and spoke into the darkened doorway. 'You called for me.' Pleasant resonating with calm authority, Marcus was pleased that his unease didn't manifest through his voice. 'How may I assist?'

A fierce force gripped his throat and pulled him close, fetid breath engulfed him and dreadful darkness grew before him, words hissed forth, viperously.

'Imbecile, you can't assist us at all. You are going to be

eviscerated, with your entrails used to strangle your successor, your sweetmeats fed to your friends at a party to celebrate your death. Before that pleasure you will face the darkest night of your vile life when all you fear will infest your being, consuming your sanity from within. Such are the plans we have for you, plans to harm you and shred your very life and visit damnation on all you love and hold dear. Before we begin, tell us why!'

'Why, what?' Marcus managed to croak, regaining something of his spirit. He might have been caught off guard by the speed of the assault and the depth of darkness that he confronted, but he was Marcus and he was not about to scared by shadows. 'Get off me, you vile creature, have you any idea who you're assaulting!'

'You would threaten me! You worm, you don't yet realise the knife has cut you through; you wriggle uselessly when in fact you are as good as dead. Before the force of life leaves your miserable form tell us why.' The darkness reshaped itself to suggest the outline of a face with piercing eyes staring out from a deeply hooded cowl.

Marcus gazed in awe as the features grew out of the night. Now a strong jaw, strong white teeth, now an aquiline nose and almost albino blond hair with eyebrows and lashes that matched. Indigo blue eyes at first cold lifeless with dark pupils suddenly flaring into animated life. The whole process of emerging from darkness to light took a matter of heartbeats, rapid panicking heartbeats that thundered on Marcus's chest. Never had he experienced such a transition from intangible to tangible, a materialisation of another-worldly kind. More than the manner of the appearance, the likeness of the face before him to one Marcus knew startled him into attempting to speak again.

'Dan! You look like Dan, you could be Dan, only more so! He's gone, disappeared from our building. Is that why I'm here and you're threatening me so vilely? I've done nothing to harm him!'

Brain now racing, Marcus looked for angles, ideas to create exits from this terrible situation. *Could this creature before him be from beyond the Borderlands, somehow evading security? Had it destroyed or imprisoned the controllers? Were there more of these things; was it in some way linked to Dan?*

Marcus knew he must win back the initiative and so decided on a strategy which he rapidly put into action. Seeking to ease the grip around his throat, he spoke. 'I don't know why Dan has disappeared, or indeed if it is him you seek. I do know that I can't help you find those answers here but let me go and I will use the full weight of my powers to find him.'

If Marcus had hoped to impress with his offer, he failed. The grip tightened. 'Your life will leave you painfully, Marcus, and the more you bluster the longer its leaving shall take. We know where Dan is, we have him, he is one of ours. We want to know why. Why you have placed him with the Elder, why you have pumped him full of poison that leaves him passionless, why you seek the lost translations. More than anything else to know who else knows. When we have the answers we seek, we want your face and your eye.'

Terror loosened Marcus's bowels, wide-eyed as the wickedly curved blade rose towards his face and journeyed incising from earlobe to chin before rising towards his eye socket. Marcus's pain and shame flowed, filling the room. Incapable of response to insistent questioning, Marcus felt himself slipping into an unreality, shock rising to defend him against the terror of the night. Silence did little to protect him as malevolent entities emerged from the shadows, many rough hands tossed him forwards and backwards. Marcus cried out in a confusion of pain and fear, and the contents of his stomach erupting, his legs failing him, he sank into a midden of his own making.

Finding his voice at last, he sought mercy. 'Please, help me. I don't know what's happening, what have I done?!' His piteous cries halted the work of the blade. 'We will help you, Marcus, we have long worked to help you rise to where you are now. You have failed us, but perhaps you can still be of use.'

Somewhere in the deeper recesses of Marcus's mind there was a recognition of the voice speaking to him. It had been a whisper, a friendly suggestion, the offer of help, in more recent times a stronger insistence for certain actions had become the dominant tone. Marcus felt so dreadfully weary he simply wanted all the torment to go away. Before passing into the eager embrace of Phobos and Deimos he willingly agreed to do as he was asked. Then the blade returned.

8

'Ice. The door is secured by a vertical bolt which sits on the inside frame dropping into the staple on the door. It is an old, but crudely effective, piece of security. As it can only be operated from the inside we are supposed to think Hanok shot the bolt. If you fill the staple with ice with the bolt ready to drop, prevented by the ice until it melts, it is simply a matter of time. There are residual traces of excess water directly beneath the door.'

Frumentus straightened and turning to Shylock gruffly thanked him for excellent work. He examined the crafty piece of subterfuge.

'I wonder why someone would want to throw suspicion onto you, Hanok? Paper copies of books, ravaged, bolts and bits of ice masking Dan's disappearance and some ancient text; it all gets very confusing. The key question is where is the boy and why would someone take him? From what you've surmised it seems he went out of that door, so we must follow.'

On the far side of the door, Frumentus felt at home. Here was modern sleek efficiency, cream-coloured walls stretched in both directions, detectors for vibration, sound, heat and movement kept a passive aggressive eye on things. Nothing could get past undetected. Except, of course something had.

Frowning, Frumentus disappeared into his inner world of doubt; how could someone get past these detectors? The only blind spot in the system was that which the great Hanok had insisted upon, namely a clear zone between his library and the first sensor of twelve feet, '*to maintain the illusion, at least, of a private space where I can study in my library*' as Hanok had explained to all who would listen. And of course, he was Hanok the Elder and he got his way, aided not least by the destruction of the main book depository.

Frumentus sunk a little lower into his gloom; '*it's not that I don't trust the technology – just the technicians*'. Hanok's words continued to circulate in his mind. Now looking at the result of that acquiescence, 12 feet of mystery, how did a boy disappear through glass walls or glass paving? The three stood side by side in silence.

Frumentus's questioning continued, echoing down the sanitised corridor.

'If they couldn't get past the detectors or pass through the walls or floor, either they are still in your library or they flew upwards. There are no signs of life within so let's see what's above us. Shylock, are you able to detect anything of interest above our heads?'

Frumentus knew the entire complex was a vast cube of intricate engineering, replete with service ducts and maintenance corridors, so perhaps there was a way to those areas from here. For many hours he had paced the quiet corridors and thoroughfares mainly devoid of noise, colour and life. He recalled how synths wordlessly passed him with slight acknowledgement, their daily routines efficiently in hand. The elect of the Citadel secure, for the main part reclining in their pods, transcending life in the raw.

'It looks like there are some faint traces of hand rails, tiny holes that you could perhaps slide climbing spikes into and work your way up. I can't compute if they'd bear much weight,' Shylock reported after a brief pause.

'They are mine,' said Hanok quietly, 'I have used them in times past to slip away undetected, when I've wanted to pass unnoticed to the Borderlands.'

Consternation spread across Frumentus's face like a rash or a slap mark. 'You mean to say you scale, what, forty to fifty feet up a sheer wall undetected and then just pop out for a spot of sunbathing! I can't quite take that in. Why not just submit the usual paperwork if you want to go out there?'

As he shifted from one foot to another, Hanok's discomfiture grew. He instinctively liked Frumentus, he needed help in the quest to find the boy and the writings.

He had understood from the outset that an option for the thieves would be his secret way and now there seemed no point in hiding its existence. Hanok was not going to give the real reason for the highly unorthodox existence of the steps. 'It is just my little way of keeping some independence, without everyone knowing my coming and going. That way I can see life as it is, not as people wish to present it to me. If you're game we can go up and see if there are indeed signs of life.'

Within a matter of minutes, the three were equipped and ready to ascend the wall. As he began to climb, Hanok called back, 'Don't be too hard on yourself, Frumentus, these climbing holes predate you by some ages. Security back then was far more interested in preventing people getting into the Citadel; they never really had a category for those who might want to leave. Why would they? This is said to be Paradise, which is a very ancient concept indeed, one I would be delighted to explore with you.'

Fearing Hanok was about to launch into the explanation and etymology of Paradise, Frumentus and Shylock took a smart step towards the wall with clear intentions to set to work ascending the heights. For a moment, Hanok watched them climb, stumped in his desire to offer further explanation of this most interesting of words. Sensing a lack of interest from his audience, the older man harrumphed under his breath.

It was surprisingly easy to locate the footholds in the walling, invisible to the eye but yielding to touch, as generous cavities emerged as the climbers ascended, Hanok lithely leading the way. With a deft flick of the wrist Hanok slid a panel of roof soundlessly away to reveal a maintenance shaft into which he climbed without visible strain.

A strong sinewy brown arm with a surprisingly firm grip grasped Frumentus, hoisting him up over the lip with Shylock. Making the transition from vertical to horizontal, the three were once again standing side by side, peering along the wide ducting. 'There are traces here, sir. A number have come this way burdened with a body, however with the exception of that body the signs are not showing themselves to be human.'

'Synths?' Hanok's expression looked like he knew the answer to that question; he had visibly paled and taken on the almost haunted look of one whose darker fears were emerging.

Shylock continued after further analysis. 'Not synths, these are living creatures, not a life as we can categorise. I can say what they are not, not what they are.'

Frumentus was witnessing the first ever failure in knowledge in Shylock, and with gleeful pleasure he sought to exploit it. 'Well, how long ago did whatever it is pass this way? Did they have the boy with them? Which way did they go, can we follow them – should we follow them?'

Shylock stared steadily ahead; 'two days have passed, yes, the boy was with them. As to whether we follow the unknown creatures into unknown cavities, that's your decision – sir.'

9

Warily, Dan lifted his head in an attempt to stretch the aching neck muscles. He didn't know how long he'd sat in the darkness, his head hanging heavily. He suspected many hours had passed since the last interview.

The rhythm of these encounters had remained unchanged; a voice carried on sweet breath had spoken invisibly behind him whilst in front were displayed many images of females in various poses and states of dress. Always the same questions about desire and attraction.

'Are you stirred by what you see? Are they not gorgeous? Are you not engorged?' It went on and on, sometimes growing in frustration and perhaps confusion that Dan seemed incapable of the response that sweet breath wanted.

Never had he felt a physical attraction to anybody else, why would he? Such things were dealt with chemically, fellow humans were to be respected for who they were; to objectify them was a heinous crime.

Now sweet breath had left Dan alone for what felt like the longest time, and he hoped that this unfathomable nightmare might come to an end. He had a clear recollection of the Elder's study, the frustration with word lists and the angry challenging words spoken.

Dan had watched as Hanok had subsided into sleep in his deep wing-backed leather chair where he stirred fitfully from time to time. He distinctly saw himself turning from the word lists to the first of the books, not so dauntingly large it couldn't be attempted. Cracking open the crusty cover he'd discovered the title *Enoch*. The pages had fallen open, yielding a sweet fragrance, the scent that rose to fill his mind and body with a deep darkness.

Dan groaned in painful frustration; he was tired of the chair and the straps and the darkness and the questions. He was hungry and thirsty and ached in places he never knew it was possible to ache. He was also angry, a sensation not experienced apart from in Hanok's study. This emotion was raw, and untested, a new thing to Dan whose life to date had been unimpeded. He wasn't sure what to do with the feelings that arose somewhere down in the depths of his being. He recalled Hanok's counsel that 'anger in itself isn't wrong, it's what you do with the anger you feel, de-couple it from violence, my boy, that's the key.'

A noise of shuffling broke into Dan's semiconscious recollections. The sound of a dragging foot and the clank of metal accompanied a muttering that was punctuated with a sucking of slobber or deep sniffing of the perpetually running nose.

'We's here with food,' came a guttural voice in the darkness. 'We's been told that you'se are to eat food, all food, leave none. Be a good boy, a kind boy and eat this.' A bowl of white puffed produce came into view, proffered by a pale hand that emerged from a dark cloak. Dan struggled to speak from a parched throat. 'Thank you, I will try, but I need a drink, I am thirsty.' Puzzled, the voice from the darkness tried again. 'We's here with food, you'se must eat all the food. Look, it's nice food, see.' A second hand with a spoon agitated the contents that rustled as they were moved. 'Good, yes? Come eat, you'se be stronger when you'se eat.'

'I will try some food, thank you,' croaked Dan, 'but first I need to drink, please help me.'

10

From within the darkness, Turiel looked at Dan, perplexed. No one had said anything about drinking, only eating. Humans ate for energy, that was known, but what was the purpose of drinking?

He tried again. 'We's here with food…' This time Dan's growing anger, firmly coupled with violence, crashed into the room. 'I said I need a drink! For pity's sake get me some water, let me drink so I can chew and swallow!'

Lashing out with his legs, Dan caught the bowl, sending it flying away into the outer darkness. A stunned silence engulfed Turiel. His hand throbbing from the kick, he looked at the boy with reproachful sad eyes filled with incomprehension.

'We's brought food and you'se hurt us. Nasty boy, Turiel just doing what he's told. 'Give the boy food; keep him safe we'll be back later.' Poor Turiel going to be in trouble now, Turiel hates boy, horrid creature, strange creature rude and nasty.'

With his helpful jailor descending into distress, Dan regretted not heeding Hanok's anger management advice and tried to make amends by croaking an apology.

Sniffling somewhat self-righteously, Turiel decided the boy was truly, deeply sorry and had, after all, had a very difficult time of it. He limped off to scrape up the spilled contents of the bowl before looking for water. Returning soon after and stepping shyly into the light, Turiel presented the bowl and a cup of water to Dan. 'I'm afraid I will need to be untied to drink and eat.'

'No, Turiel isn't to let you go. If you run Turiel is in trouble. Poor Turiel, he can't go with them because he is lame. Turiel never gets to go with them, he's always here watching in the dark, he misses the light and the fun, but he can't go back, poor Turiel.'

Reaching out tenderly, Turiel placed a cup to Dan's lips. Gratefully Dan drank. Again the cup was offered and Dan drank. Then a spoonful of white fluff made its unsteady approach to Dan's lips. Hesitating at first and then with growing relish, Dan ate spoonful after spoonful. 'This is delicious, thank you, Turiel, I've never tasted food like this, what is it?'

'Oh this,' said Turiel, 'this? This is nothing, it's just the food of us angels.'

11

Along the service shaft, the three crept as quietly as they could, the clear smell of recycled air leading. 'Just by here,' Hanok pointed. 'I would slip through the cowling when the fans stopped as they did every ten minutes on the hour. Perhaps your security needs tightening, Frumentus.'

With a twinkle in his eye Hanok eased past the solid presence of Frumentus to catch up with Shylock. 'We've travelled the thirty minutes or so it takes me to reach the outside, Shylock, does the trail lead us away from the building?'

Shylock's analysis was as alarming as it was analytical, causing deep alarm. 'Frumentus, you will know if they've fled via the acoustic drivers Dan's in serious trouble. No one can survive there for long.' Concern was writ large on the faces of the two.

Shylock sighed inwardly; *well state the obvious, why not, let's all join in shall we..?* 'I'm aware of the risk for humans, it's even greater for synths, we are most likely to malfunction after the briefest of exposure, maybe fifteen minutes by my calculation. Humans might survive longer but with long term side effects to be expected. Given that Dan's captors are other than human it does represent a perfect lair.' Shylock might have been said to have expressed a grudging respect for this as yet uncategorised life form, but of course that would be most unlike a synth.

The three stood with uncertainty dogging two of them. To go on was hazardous; to go back seeking help was an abandonment of Dan. Whatever the intention of his captors he could not survive in the deafening chamber. Too much depended on the delicate acoustic balance being maintained for the drive to be reduced, if it were, Citadel would sink towards the volatile earth that had specifically been cleared of all signs of humanity. Nothing could be permitted that would interfere with the flow of the sound waves. The life of one would not justify decreasing the drive, just as the lives of many prevented their creation.

'Look here, Frumentus, I'm the one who is most closely associated with Dan, he was under my tutelage and care when whatever happened. I must press on towards the drivers. You don't need to put yourselves in harm's way. Someone must report the presence of these creatures in the heart of the Citadel, who knows what their intentions are? If I am lucky I may yet find Dan in time to bring him out.'

Frumentus was touched by Hanok's fearless heartfelt compassion for the boy, and suddenly he knew that destiny was calling to him, here today at this place and time. 'It is for a time such as this that I took on this position. I'm Head of Security when there's nothing to secure. I suffer mockery behind my back, and at times in front of my face. Well, all that fades to dust now. A real crime has occurred, and real danger confronts the Citadel. I can't leave you to face this alone, Hanok, not if I ever want to look myself in the mirror again. I will be with you in this. Shylock, we need your tracker to keep up the pursuit and we need you, please, to take a report back directly to Head of the Corporation, Marcus, as swiftly as you can.'

Stepping purposely forward, Frumentus felt for the first time a certainty that he was doing the right thing, for the right reasons and in the right way. Hanok glanced at Shylock before setting out to follow the rolling gait of the head of security.

‘Sir.’ The voice of Shylock sounded almost mournful. ‘Shall I return once the message is delivered?’

‘Yes, but will you be able to follow us past this point without the tracker? You’re vulnerable to the acoustic drives. Don’t put yourself at risk of enduring damage, your evidence may be vital to the Citadel.’

‘I will upload a full report of events to date prior to returning. Sir, please be careful in your quest. I am charged with your protection, with the risk factors as high as this, your enterprise has a high probability of harm to you.’

Smiling, Frumentus turned to face the unknown future. ‘Anyone would think he cared,’ he muttered to himself. Then more clearly he called, ‘Thank you, Shylock, I intend to return.’

12

'They should have looked up.' Spiro kicked the crushed hulk of the Landy contemptuously.

'They should but they never do.' Zenobia regarded the effects of the rock fall with a mixture of satisfaction and sorrow. It had been a good plan, luring the troop carrier to a place of destruction, a success in the endless fighting, yet looking at the broken corpses butchered by wild-eyed followers, Zenobia felt the heat of battle drain from her.

'They're just children, somebody's sons, somebody's daughters, alive no more.' As she stepped delicately around the carnage, Zenobia picked out from the detritus of death a scattered mix of personal possessions. They were of no interest to looting hands but to Zenobia they were reminders of life now caught in the evening breeze.

Zenobia spoke mainly to herself as she gathered fragments of life. 'Truly, we are but grass that grows up only to wither and perish, there has to be more to life than death.' A picture caught her eye and stooping to pick it up, she gasped. The image was a family scene; proud parents with what looked like a newly qualified dragoon, her arms casually draped around the shoulders of her parents. The sight was unusual, as so few parents saw their children grow to adult life, so she guessed this was one of the mercenaries. Few from the

Citadel offered service in Borderlands when serving time in Home Defence Force.

The picture of family life instantly and unexpectedly took Zenobia back to her own parents. In that scene there were no smiles, only screams and flames and the noise of destruction. Even now, Zenobia could feel the intensity of the heat on her skin, could smell the burning human flesh filling her nose. Choking, desperate cries filled her ears as parents inhaled smoke and flame. Death came cruelly. It was the stuff of nightmares for the child Zenobia. The family had been one of many sheltering in their timbered sanctuary waiting for the all clear to be sounded from yet another raid. Overhead the drones were excessively active. 'Surely peace will come soon,' were her father's reassuring words to her, as her mother embraced them both, squeezing that bit tighter, as if she doubted it would ever be so.

'We're just in the wrong place at the wrong time. The Citadel will understand this is our land too. We've been here generations, this is our home. We shall not be moved easily. They must be reasonable.'

But they weren't. By some sleight of hand the Telemeric Corporation's grip on the secrets of endless life empowered the Citadel. Their right to all the land over which they intended their creation to float received international recognition; it was, after all, an ancient right that they claimed and all who occupied 'their' land would not be permitted to stay, it was '*for the greater good*'.

The clearances were ruthless. When the wind was blowing hard from the east, fires were set that saw the ancient timbers burst into flame almost immediately, then the fire fed on itself and swept through the settlement with a fierce intensity that left no hope of escape for those in its path. Desperate hands that no longer squeezed reassuringly shoved Zenobia through the smallest of doorways down into the deep cellar, with the heavy door slammed shut over her head.

The roaring and screaming lasted an eternity, the smell seeped into her pores. Emerging later, maybe hours or maybe days, to nothing but blackened remains and windblown ash, Zenobia was seemingly reborn into a darkness that gripped her arising from a scene of the barbaric destruction of innocence.

The giant form of Spiro came and stood alongside his leader, sensing the sorrow settling upon her and wanting to affirm the rightness of their work. Spiro turned to Zenobia and gazed fiercely into her eyes.

'I see your sorrow at these deaths, that's natural, for you are meant to be a bringer of life, not its destroyer. You are our leader, Zenobia. Lead us through warfare to a time when life will mean more than surviving day by day on the very edge of the world whilst others live endlessly.'

Zenobia broke the grip to look at the desolation surrounding her. Before, perched high above the machine, willing for the rocks to fall, she had felt the familiar fierce hatred towards the Citadel. Down in the valley, the feeling faded.

'Spiro, I am weary of all this. I want to see the Citadel killed, not these children. We need to get to the very core of its being and stop its life force; anything less is pointless.'

'We shall have our victory, Zenobia; you shall have your rest. But for now we must leave this place, we've stripped what we can from the machine. Mostly it's ruined but some armaments have been taken, the driver still lives but not for long.'

'He lives? I did not know. How did anyone survive such a crushing? The driver must be made of toughened metal.' Ignoring the stench Zenobia eased into the cockpit where, gazing mutely at a still swinging charm as monitors flickered hissing their pain, lay a rock-pierced Dromas.

'You'll bleed out before help can come. Yours will be a slow death in a cold desert far from friends. I could try and save you but then you'd be my creature, what is it to be? Will you live for me, trooper, or would you die for the Citadel?'

'Zenobia, the drones are coming! Kill him if you want to but hurry!' Spiro's voice reached to her as she crouched inches from the trooper within the broken vehicle. Not understanding her own conflicted desire yet certain that in some way her destiny would be shaped by this broken man, she waited.

Dromas was in a state of deep shock. The fierce woman before him offered him life and he wanted life. He chose life before losing consciousness.

Deep within his mind the image of the dark-eyed woman was with him, calling him to hang on, assuring him 'all will be well, all will be well, all is well – rest, my Sergeant Dromas.'

13

The pursuit led Frumentus and Hanok to the base of the Citadel, and what was the first in a series of heavy blast doors which represented the beginning of the secure zone containing and directing the acoustic drivers. The magnetically sealed doors of the security system barred any further progress.

'Each series of doors can only be activated by code.' Frumentus spoke with wonderment. 'Whoever is ahead of us is well informed or possesses technology in advance of mine that can release the doors. However, being Head of Security has some advantages!' Frumentus's efforts rewarded by the hiss of hydraulics opening the vast doors as the magnetic seal was disabled. 'In we go.'

Intense vibrations assaulted their senses as an invisible force pressed down on their shoulders whilst pounding their heads with spiked hammer blows. Headaches and dizziness gripped the couple as they staggered forward, eyes watering. High above in the vaulted ceiling the vibrating machines pulsated sound waves towards the external amplification system at the exact frequency and intensity to float the complex on a sea of sound.

Heat exchange units kept the temperature at safe operating levels, with the vast spaces around the chamber acting as both a coolant and amplification chamber for the energy released. It was a vast sounding drum, a beating heart that kept the Citadel aloft.

Frumentus was visibly sagging with the intensity of the vibrations as Hanok grasped his shoulder and shoved him forward. 'We've got to get across the chamber quickly! No one can survive in here more than a short time, they must have taken Dan across at a great pace!'

Hanok looked grimly out on the vast chamber that spread out before him. If Dan was alive it would be a miracle, He only hoped the journey through this place had been swift for the lad or that he'd been unconscious.

The two pressed forward as if they were pushing into the face of a wall of resistance. As time went on, the rhythmic waves of pain increasingly pulsated through them causing each to stagger down onto their knees, then rise and press on only to stagger and fall again.

The erratic progress continued for what felt like an eternity, but eventually the weight of the force field pushed them down flat onto the floor. It was intense beyond endurance. Frumentus felt something wet running out of his ears and realised they were bleeding.

On and on went the pounding, merciless and indifferent to the cries of two frail humans crawling forward to escape the fearsome place.

Hanok refused to be crushed. He inched towards the far side of the hall where he thought he saw what appeared to be the exit. Dragging Frumentus's head closer, Hanok frantically signalled towards the opening. 'Over there!'

Frumentus, quite incapable of hearing and utterly unprepared for the pain, was sinking back into a world of confusion and self-doubt. The old voices reasserted themselves just as loudly and as pressingly as anything the acoustic field could achieve, equally deadly to Frumentus. He was a fool, not a hero, what was he doing in this dreadful place? Hanok was shouting at him again, shaking him and pointing towards the far wall but it made no sense. His vision blurring, ears bleeding, Frumentus began to curl into the foetal position just wanting it to stop. He'd failed again, Frumentus the Fool; *give up, fool curl up and die, you are useless, you always have been and always will be useless.*

Dragging the immobile Frumentus by his arms, Hanok gasped as he inched his way across the floor, shuffling backwards on his backside, gaining what purchase he could with his feet. Mercifully the pressure was easing as they edged towards the exit.

'Come on, Frumentus! Help yourself, we're almost there, get going, man!'

In frustration Hanok dropped the arms of the inert man and began slapping his face harder and harder until, cheeks stinging, Frumentus opened a groggy eye and screamed in deep animal pain. A sensation of life returning to his limbs now engulfed the hapless Frumentus in an intensified and macabre version of pins and needles, causing the massive flow of blood through him as pressure eased from the terrible acoustic forces. He rose, scrabbling legs propelling him forward in a desperate attempt to escape this new torture. With arms flailing he knocked Hanok aside and staggered in the direction of the hatch. Gaining speed Frumentus charged, head down towards sanctuary, and rammed himself head first into the wall to the left of the hatch. Hanok, breathing deeply, edged across to the poleaxed policemen and having satisfied himself there were signs of life he grunted in satisfaction and began the process of dragging him through the door.

14

Hurrying back along the passage, Shylock attempted to contact Marcus via the secure coms without success. He had reported on the daily round of security work Frumentus undertook on a regular basis ever since his commission. The work had seemed very mundane, routine and uneventful, but the reporting of his movements and manner was 'essential' according to Marcus who had a very particular interest in the man. Like all synths under the industry protocols, he was unable to harm a human physically; indeed, he was to protect life, but he was able to report fully on their actions. Synths couldn't be soldiers, but they made good servants, and on occasions, excellent spies.

Marcus needed a spy, for Frumentus was his fool, that much Shylock knew. He calculated that some of the disasters surrounding the loss of the library, although laid at Frumentus's door, had Marcus's hand behind them. A certain arrogance and disrespect had been programmed into the synth, ensuring all Frumentus's follies were reported back with no juicy details left out. However most recently, really since the adventure with Hanok had begun, a change had come over Frumentus, new life and purpose surrounded him. Most troublingly this had not been reported back as Shylock had lost contact with his master. He would have preferred to stay with Frumentus and Hanok in their mysterious pursuit, but the clear order from Frumentus and the lack of contact with Marcus meant he had no choice but to go.

Soon he was at the wall of Hanok's library and easily scaled down to the floor. Within a short time Shylock had made his way through to the main offices of the Corporation and was asking to see Marcus, only to discover access denied and security officers in front of his door.

Shylock needed to relay his information and he urgently needed to get back to the search. Following the 'Hanok solution' he sought the service shaft through which the lifeblood of the Citadel flowed. It was remarkably easy to climb into the warren of ducting and to soundlessly move along it. Now it became a simple task to navigate his way to the office suite and drop into the main boardroom undetected.

Once inside Shylock took careful bearings, not wanting to disturb whatever important discussions were being held. Sliding back the cover on the service shaft to leave no clue of how he entered, Shylock padded from room to room, looking for Marcus. The entire suite was devoid of life; whatever had been here was no longer. Shylock stood in the inner sanctum, next to the vaults which contained the codes to unlock the Citadel's control systems. The vault doors themselves, however, were ajar, and within Shylock could see something lying discarded on the floor. At this range, his detectors couldn't instantly recognise what he was seeing. In time the focus came. In the nerve centre of the organisation lay a substantial part of the face, including the shrivelled eyeball, of Marcus Dromas, head of the Telemeric Corporation, and leader of the Citadel. Synths aren't given to emotional outbursts, but from time to time human phrases enter their vocabulary that could be thought of as expressing strong feelings, 'Oh shit' being one such example.

15

Gaining entry to the Citadel had not been difficult, its citizens were secure in their superiority and lax in their defence as they had powerful allies willing to spring to their defence – in return for access to the Citadel's life-extending knowledge. Samyaza led them through the ground to air portals, their movements obscured by cloaking magic. The difficulty had been to keep the flesh, and particularly the eye, of Marcus fresh enough to use. A thick enough slice of jowl folded onto and behind the orb where some of Armaros's solution had worked well. Once the party was securely in the Directors' suite Marcus's features and facts eagerly yielded access to the prize codes.

For many years Marcus had been of interest to the Watchers. Lurking within the shadowy world of the external controllers, they used their influence to aid Marcus's rise to power, first within the Corporation and later the Citadel. The Watchers extended their influence over the mind of Marcus, recognising his usefulness to them. The task of moulding his thoughts to their will was made easier as Marcus was, at heart, a petulant juvenile used to getting his own way by whatever means. He loved having power over people, rather than using that power for them. The prestige and all that came with it, especially the control over the lives of others, was his dark delight. Notions of deity appealed to an ego that could not face the possibility that he might be in error on any given subject. Any truth that didn't fit with his truth was simply falsehood, at best a misspeaking, at worst, a personal affront to be crushed.

Marcus's narcissism was encouraged, as his way to leadership was cleared in both Corporation and Citadel by the Watchers. By the time he arrived in the role he had long desired, he was almost unknowingly entirely their creature.

The greatest challenge to Marcus had been Hanok, a stubborn force of resistance to all the Watchers desired. By rights, he should have been Director, but his plans to offer universally the benefit of endless life to all peoples, rather than just citizens of the Citadel had been fiercely resisted by the Convocation.

The Watchers had both planted the seed of the idea of such largesse and encouraged the successful opposition to such plans, forcing Hanok to stand aside, thus making him the best leader the Corporation never had.

Once in place Marcus had worked to ensure more powers gravitated towards him. A programme of geographical desolation was put in force in order to protect the Corporation from external threats. Terror attacks were staged to destabilise the Citadel and inculcate fear of those 'out there'. Memories of the violent shaking of the earth that had destroyed so many communities and cities were retold endlessly, feeding the narrative of fear to a people who lived safely above the shaking earth. The Border force was established to 'get our retaliation in first', and the might of the Citadel began to turn from the preservation of life to the termination of the life of 'others'. All was done in the name of protecting 'us' from those who wanted 'our way of life', to take the secrets and destroy all that was good about 'our life together'. Fear fed on anxieties, and in the shadows the Watchers continued their work to see humanity turn in on itself with destructive defiance.

Marcus had been a successful pawn in the greater game that was afoot, but he'd erred. His greatest failure had been to allow Dan to fall into the clutches of Hanok, the one person who could unmask the Watchers. Exposure was their great fear. How Hanok had discovered Dan confounded and enraged Samyaza; he was certain Marcus was playing a double game. Swift action had followed. First snatching Dan and the writings, before assaulting the Citadel directly.

Aware of the risks he was running, Samyaza left the room without glancing down at Marcus's face, past the entranced guards. Satisfying himself all was as he wanted, he whispered to the senior sergeant that none were to enter, and he sealed the door.

Samyaza exited the Citadel for the depths of the external control room whence he had emerged not more than an hour previously. 'Do we do well in this, Samyaza?' Zarak's eye gazed steadily at his leader as they spoke telepathically. 'Is it wise to break the boundaries set by above? Will not wrath follow as surely as judgement?'

Samyaza bristled. 'What choice do we have? Events are moving fast and we can't afford to lose control of all we have prepared. It is within the order of things that we test and push these creatures towards the boundaries, it is for them to resist or not.'

Did they do well? Yes, in that the situation was under control. Dan was with them, his detoxification under way. Yes the writings had been, albeit unsubtly, removed and with them the risk of their discovery. Samyaza didn't know if that was a matter of random chance or the work of a higher guiding-hand that had caused Hanok to amass so many writings virtually unnoticed.

'At least we haven't killed, have we, Zarak? If we had then most certainly boundaries that should not be crossed would have been breached, and who knows what trouble would come our way. No one was killed this day, even Marcus lives, in a manner of speaking.'

16

'What do you mean, angel food?' Dan looked enquiringly from the proffered bowl to Turiel. He bit into another piece of the candy-like substance. The texture was both firm and crunchy, yet it disappeared on the tongue, making swallowing rather unnecessary. Despite that, Dan was feeling quite full after a bowlful of the food, washed down with fresh water, and his energy levels and curiosity were rising.

'I've never heard of angel food, let alone tasted it before; does it have any other name?' Turiel looked at the bowl and then at Dan, uncertain whether to give it the other name.

'Whatsit,' he mumbled.

'I asked what is it called, this angel food of yours?' Dan repeated the question.

'Whatsit,' Turiel replied.

Slowly Dan tried again. 'The food I am eating, does it have another name? I love all things culinary and I've eaten just about every dish known to man, but I have never come across this.'

That really did startle Turiel: whoever heard of a Nephilim being lovingly interested in food? He looked at Dan and wondered, not for the first time, if he really was as Samyaza said, one of the few remaining ones. 'Angel food is our name for it. It's also known as 'Whatsit' and the story goes that when it came down from the heavens people ate and asked 'what is it?' and the name stuck, or rather the translation of their speech stuck, for translated it sounds like 'manna'.

'Came down from where? Heaven, that sounds like one of the stories Hanok told.'

Turiel realised he had disclosed too much information already. He shuddered to think what might befall him if the others found out. Eyes welling with tears and fear, he stuttered, 'Please don't go talking about Heaven. We's be punished terribly.'

Dan leaned as far forward as the restraints would allow and spoke to reassure. 'Thank you for your kindness. I've enjoyed the manna. Its taste and your words resonate deep within my memory. If you can please tell me more.'

Encouraged, Turiel threw caution to the wind and began to speak rapidly. 'We's so glad your memories are stirring. We's tried to reach you but their poison quench desire and you've been lost to us even though you're one of us.'

'I've no idea who you are. I can trace my family line through the records office well enough, so how is it you speak as though I'm linked to you?' Dan drew back in his confusion.

Turiel knew there was no holding back now; the doorway into Dan's mind was swinging slightly open and he, Turiel, least of them all, was the one there to push it fully open. 'Generations ago we's watched the daughters of Adam from afar. They were beautiful, gorgeous and we desired them greatly. Their softened skin, the swell of their breasts, the light in their eyes, their laughter and love, all played upon us, called to us, drew us away from His side, until we's knew we's must possess them. So, we crossed the un-crossable divide to woo the women with magic and mind tricks. We taught them well and we shared their bodies. Two hundred came, now we're scattered amongst the shadows of the earth.'

Dan saw truth in the deformed creature in front of him. That there even were such things as angels and Heaven stretched credulity, but then to leave Heaven just to have sex, by all accounts a highly overrated and wasteful means of pleasure and reproduction seemed even more unlikely.

'I don't understand why you'd want to travel just for that but be that as it may, where do I fit into your story? Where's our shared history?'

Now with a triumphant gleam in his eye the little Watcher sucked in the saliva that was beginning to flow freely, not as before from anxiety, but for the fact that the pinnacle of the story was being reached. 'We's married the daughters of Adam, and the fruit of that union are people like you. Dan, 'the Nephilim' they were called. Giants, heroes of ancient times, mighty in valour, skilled in the arts, workers of metal and stone, great builders of pyramids and all manner of wonders in the ancient world. We's created a new breed, greater than humans, different from angels. Once there were many of you powerful in this very land dominating humanity, but then He interfered.

'The floodwaters came carrying all before it, crushing, drowning, mangling. My own feet were shattered, my arm crushed, but I am a Watcher and I can't be killed. We hid in the dark places, watched and waited and worked in the shadows towards the final solution, a time when the Nephilim will rise to stride the earth.'

Dan rocked back in the chair, recoiling from the torrent of invective that had flowed from his captor. His demeanour changed from mildly servile and incompetent, seemingly growing in size and menace, his voice had taken on a power and force that rose from deep dark places. It was almost the voice of another speaker, with Turiel the manikin giving temporary residence to it as if he were possessed by a malignancy.

Never had Dan experienced the presence of such a powerful void drawing him towards the edge of the frightening darkness, an all-consuming hatred. 'You see, all the earth belongs to you, Dan. With my help you can take possession of it. I only ask that you follow me obediently, and I will give you your heart's desires.'

The powerful voice rumbled ominously around the room, booming off the craggy walls, assaulting Dan's senses, causing them to vibrate at the deepest levels. Then it was gone and Turiel was speaking. 'We's want you back, Dan. We's will help you to feel desire again for the women. We's will share our secrets with you, we's will show you who you really are.'

'No!' cried Dan. 'Don't!' but it was too late. Turiel looked into Dan's astonished eyes to find they weren't focused on him at all but staring behind him. 'No, don't, he's harmless, he's much to tell me, I need to hear what he has to say.' Sensing danger, Turiel leapt upwards and flung himself as far to the right as his crippled legs would allow. Landing painfully, he nevertheless came up from a crouching stance ready to spring. With a shriek, he launched himself at the two forms that were advancing upon him, preparing to tear and bite.

'Steady now.' The calming voice carried authority but no fear of Turiel. 'We're after our friend here. We don't know who you are, but we don't want to hurt you, we just want to help him.' One of the two figures was extending a placatory hand towards Turiel, while the other stood, hands returning to rest at his side.

'No. you can't take him; he's ours. We's to look after him until they get back, it won't be long before they do, and then you will be sorry you ever came here.' The figures were coming closer to Dan. Turiel knew that he would lose his boy just when he reached him. Piteously he let out a moan of despair; 'they'se will hurt poor Turiel, when they find the boy gone. Poor Turiel, poor, poor Turiel.'

Large mournful eyes looked up at the figures now standing over Dan 'Please don't take him, he's all we's have.' Turiel's words had failed to deter the two from advancing ever closer to Dan, so he sprang. 'Leave we's alone!' screamed Turiel, striking and biting with all his might. From the corner of his eye Turiel saw the other stranger raise his arm and then bring it down with a crashing force that sent Turiel into limp unconsciousness.

Gasping for breath from the shock of the attack, Frumentus flung the limp creature from his shoulders. 'What in the name of all that's good is that thing?' He looked, wild-eyed, towards Hanok still menacing the inert form with a cosh. 'I'm not at all certain, but it said there were others coming. That might be a lie but we don't want to find out, do we. Let's be quick about releasing these bindings. How are you, Dan? Have you been injured? Can you move? Dan! Can you hear me?'

Dan stared as gently Hanok reached towards him, unable to move, barely able to speak. 'Hanok, have you killed him?' Hanok's familiar appraising stare flowed over him from the depths of wisdom past.

Frumentus was busily engaged in unpicking Dan's bindings. 'Hello, I'm Frumentus, Head of Security at the Citadel, I don't think we've met. I have spent the last few hours or is it days, I lose track, trying to find and rescue you. I've nearly died heading through the acoustic drive chamber. I've crawled through some foul passageways following your traces and now been attacked by a black-hearted midget who you seem to have grown fond of, and who, before my friend here knocked him unconscious possibly killing him, told us that there are a whole bunch of similar midgets who will tear us to pieces. I really need you to get yourself together, so we can get to a place of safety where I can call in support and find just what on earth this place is and who these creatures are. Please can we go?'

Held by the gaze of Hanok, Dan remained motionless. 'What have you learnt, boy, what has been told to you? Where have you been taken to? Dan, open your mind to me let me see into your soul, child

– "soul", remember that word.' The two were locked together for what seemed an age, each drinking in the other, soul to soul, sightless.

Frumentus, in despair, cast around for some distraction, anything to encourage urgency. The creature was still, and scattered around were signs of their struggle. A bowl here, a cup there, images of women flickering on a screen the room darkened with the damp aroma of deep earth. The room seemed devoid of any objects except for a small bundle, partially wrapped. Frumentus gave a shout of triumph.

17

Scurrying silently in the moonlit shadows, the scavenger sniffed at the dried blood staining the twisted metal that mingled with the sweetly scented night air. The corpses had been removed by the drone-led recovery squad, leaving enough traces of their passing to attract others. The scene was alive with curious creatures hoping for some morsel to sustain them in the cold night. Above, perched on a rocky outcrop, the owl watched the movement below, awaiting its chance. Rising on soundless wings it swooped. A shriek, then silence as death continued to play its part in the circle of life.

Satisfied, the owl flapped silently back to its high perch. A clock ticked down the final moments and at the ordained time a vast fireball ripped through the steel hull, incinerating scavengers whilst ascending with a speed that nearly caught the owl in its heat. Shaken, it flapped away to the east, seeking quieter places.

'The troopers have destroyed it. I wonder if they timed the charge or something tripped it. Either way that's the end of that.' Spiro looked out from the cave as the remains of the fireball faded into the night, the sound reverberating around the rock walls. Zenobia didn't look up from her work of gently easing the rock shards from the unconscious Sergeant Dromas. 'Spiro, can you help me put pressure on the wound? I'm going to take the remains of the rock away and I need to staunch the flow of blood as quickly as I can.'

Coming to her side, Spiro looked down dubiously. 'You're the healer, and I've seen you work miracles with some of the lads who have been totally mangled by drone strikes and worse, but is it worth the effort of trying to save this one? He looks like a lost cause to me.'

'We must try, Spiro, I believe there is a reason he yet lives. I saw something in his eyes that craved freedom and release. Not just from the weight of the rock or the grip of death but release from his fate.'

Having dragged the trooper from the Landy, Spiro had worked with Zenobia to get the inert body up the steep track. Within moments of their disappearing over a false summit, drones filled the canyon, agitated mechanical hornets their anger at the destruction was palpable. Rounding the sheer rock face appeared impossible, but the surefooted party were intimately familiar with the track and they slipped silently along it, no more than a passing shadow, before disappearing into a near invisible crevice to safety.

Now at the back of the cave, the two worked swiftly. Leaving the horse to graze on the diminishing supply of hay, they'd stripped Sergeant Dromas of his uniform and body armour.

Upon closer inspection it was found that the rock shard had missed vital organs and blood vessels. Swiftly Zenobia removed the remaining fragments using the flickering light of the torch to guide her instinctive hands. Gently probing the area until she was satisfied all had been removed, she worked to stitch the punctured flesh, lacing it with her healing paste. 'I can't do much with broken ribs, but I hope I've done enough to stop him dying. I can pray for his recovery and we can wait and see what healing looks like for him.'

Rising to shake the stiffness from her limbs and cleanse the blood from her hands, Zenobia faced Spiro. 'Thank you again, Spiro.'

'For what?'

'Trusting me.'

Tiredness fell away from Spiro at Zenobia's words. He ached to hold this fragile flower, worn and weary from her work not only as a leader of fighters nor this day's bloodletting, but from a deeper weariness of carrying the flame of hope for his forgotten people. She stepped into his open arms and felt the warm safe embrace enfold and comfort her, for a moment taking the loneliness away.

'I was taken back to the burning today,' she whispered into his chest. 'I was that girl again surrounded by the screams of my family and many others. I survived but my heart melted in the fire that day. Now I get so cold and feel so alone, anger is frozen in me like a weight that is dragging me down.' Looking up into the face of her comforter, Zenobia felt safe, warm. 'I'm told that to be free of this weight, to live a life unburdened by the past, I have to forgive those who damaged me and destroyed my own. But I can't. When I try a darkness wells up within me. I hear their screams. I smell their flesh. I'm walking amongst their charred remains. I am alone, frightened and bitter.'

Nestling further into Spiro, Zenobia felt the comfort of soothing hands running through her hair. She listened to the deep rhythmic breathing of the man and offered up a prayer of gratitude for such a friend as this before slipping into sleep.

Unwilling to disturb her sleep Spiro remained seated, the young girl wrapped in his arms, her easy breathing reassuring him that the pain of the past was, for the moment at least, a distant place in her life.

Outside, the night creatures moved in hushed tones, the owl beat its silent wings, a sentinel surveying its domain, the flames from the Landy having long since extinguished. Sergeant Dromas stirred painfully and then settled back to sleep, the horse whinnied, a gentle hoof scuffing the dry ground. A stillness descended into the cave that even Spiro could discern, the presence of another, a safe comforting healing presence that came to make everything well, seeping into dreams of soldier and girl alike.

18

The shock of office was still numbing acting Director Davidson as he sat with the grisly presence of his predecessor contained in an airtight bag. All monitors were reading situation stable, population calm, Telemorese production continuing. The Citadel continued.

Shylock's report was efficient and dispassionate, and the conclusions jarred.

On his feet and pacing, Davidson continued to think aloud. 'Do we know anything of our adversaries, any communication from them, any idea what they want?'

Shylock considered. 'An unrecognised life force wanted the boy and they wanted a book. The same force potentially has control of the Citadel, none of it computes logically. In the face of such illogical opposition we are at high risk of catastrophic descent. We need time to secure our drivers, and the logical solution is a controlled descent and urgent reprogramming.'

Decision made, Davidson rose with serious intent, knowing what momentous decisions were now required of the emergency convocation.

'Sir, may I request the task of seeking to know the status of Director Marcus before returning to Head of Security Frumentus? I am instructed to report to him and as yet I have not completed that task. If he has succumbed to those terrible wounds, then I can close the outstanding task. If he hasn't he may become a conduit by which we can reach whoever lies behind these things.' Davidson looked at the contents of the bag and then towards the synth. He shrugged as he turned to leave

'Yes thank you, Shylock, your request is granted, but how you compute he could live through such mutilation is beyond me, there must be a pound of flesh in front of us.'

~ ~ ~

In the lonely places of the wilderness, they built them out of sight and mind. Homes to house the failures, the aged ones. It had been Marcus's solution to the unpalatable truth. No one was to be euthanized, that would be an anathema to him. Just hide them away out in the Borderlands to live out their days in quiet. Fine places of rest and enjoyment well earned by faithful servants of the Citadel. No need to remain within the confines of the community, these blessed ones would quietly be carried to another place, the failure of Telemeric Corporation hidden.

As more homes followed, the secret grew to be monstrous, taking on a life of its own, kept locked away out of sight, a gross embarrassment. A failure. The Telemeric medication inhibited death but it transpired that mutations occurred, brain synapses were inhibited and mental capacity reduced gradually, almost imperceptibly. Some people became locked into a terrifying world of loneliness. Unable to cry out or break out, they lived out endless days in mute despair. That which had been intended for their liberty became the very thing that enslaved them. Now amongst his creation Marcus lay, abandoned, horribly mutilated, scarcely able to speak. From his one remaining eye he had beheld the reality of the first of the homes. Distressed and frightened faces stared mutely past him as the trolley was wheeled along. He lay alone, guttural distress his waking companion; tortured dreams met him whenever he sank into exhausted sleep. Within the hell on earth, Marcus waited.

19

Battered and bruised by his journey as he was, Frumentus brandished aloft a battered leather-bound book with hysterical joy, saying, 'this must be it!' He hurried across to Hanok, whose gaze remained firmly fixed on the younger man. 'Look, Hanok, is this one of your precious books that we've been searching for? For goodness sake, man! Will you look or shall I throw it back into obscurity?'

Frumentus was getting increasingly panicked. The chance that a considerable host of nasty creatures were about to spew out of the darkened doorway to tear at them, as the wizened one had warned, was a frightening prospect. Equally unsettling was the trance both Hanok and Dan seemed to have slipped into, each lost in the other's eyes. Roughly shaking the older man had no effect in breaking his fixation, waving the book in his face was equally pointless.

Now the creature Hanok had coshed was beginning to stir and groan. Poor Frumentus was close to tears; he tried a slap to the face, gentle at first then harder, his hand striking Hanok's leathery skin, bouncing off to no effect.

'Come on, you old fool, snap out of it. They're coming. It's waking up. He's not moving. Do something!' Nothing. Frantically searching Hanok's pockets, Frumentus found the leather cosh. With a heavy smack Frumentus brought the cosh down on Turiel's head. Deciding the inert creature could still pose a threat, Frumentus took the loosened bindings from Dan's chair and bound Turiel's limbs.

He was casting around for a gag when he stopped; appalled, he thought he caught the sound of approaching feet coming from further doorway. 'Oh no, not now! Hanok, they're coming I can hear them. Can you hear me? Please, Hanok, whatever you're doing wherever you've gone in your mind you have to come back to me, we have to get out of here.' There was no doubt something was coming, and Frumentus considered running, going back the way he'd come but that would mean the pain of the chamber. It would also mean abandoning these two people. He had little feelings for the boy, but Hanok had become important to him, not a friend as such because Frumentus didn't really do friendship, but a colleague, and someone who had most likely saved his life.

Frumentus unconsciously ran his hands up the back of his neck and over his head, coming onto the painful lump. Hanok had hauled him through the doorway and eased him along away from the terrible forces that had so tortured and would have killed him. When he had eventually regained consciousness and realised the pain was easing, he felt overwhelming gratitude to Hanok. Now he couldn't just leave him to whatever fate was about to pour through the doorway, he wouldn't fail his companion at this time.

Energised by this conviction, Frumentus ran towards the sound of approaching danger, as a metal door unused for what must have been ages hidden in the gloom offered hope. Desperation gave Frumentus extra strength as using all his might he felt the door shift, and with loud protest begin to swing shut.

Momentum was now with Frumentus and he used it to shove the door firmly and loudly closed. It seemed to possess no locks to assist Frumentus, so he leant his weight against the door, breathing heavily, wondering what he could do next. As his breathing calmed he realised the sound of approach was gone, even with his ear up against the metal all was silent. He pressed in harder in-order to listen, nothing. He waited.

A tremendous crash against the door shattered any hope. A furious pounding beat against him. It was a pounding and not a pushing, more frustration than reason at work. Frumentus knew it couldn't last, soon whatever was on the other side would force its way in. The pounding intensified, then eased, then stopped.

Ears ringing, Frumentus felt the push come. Tentative at first, it grew, and although Frumentus pushed back with all his weight and strength he felt the door begin to move. Slowly, steadily the gap grew, and Frumentus sensed that whoever was pushing was doing so cautiously, unwilling simply to burst the door open as they were unaware of what faced them on the inside.

'It's just as well they don't know it's just me here,' he muttered to himself, eyes closed with the effort of pushing back.

'Just you, my dear friend, I think not!' The voice of Hanok washed over Frumentus in a refreshing surge of hope and joy.

'You're back! I can't keep this closed. Whatever is out there is keen to get in here and I don't think it's friendly.'

As he spoke the pressure on the door abruptly ceased, causing Frumentus to slam home the door. Hanok brought the chair that had held Dan captive and wedged it against the door before searching more thoroughly. Grunting with satisfaction, he eased a bolt across. 'There's nearly always a manual override for doors, we used to call them bolts.'

Smiling, Hanok regarded Frumentus's bedraggled state. 'Thank you, Frumentus, I know you could have left me but you didn't. You fought for my life as well as Dan's and your own. That took courage because it must have seemed a foolishly hopeless thing to do, yet you did it; 'Frumentus the Fool' no longer, 'Frumentus my friend' from now on.'

Awkwardly, Frumentus allowed himself to be caught up in an embrace that squeezed the breath from his body whilst bringing a warmth to his heart, the likes of which he'd never experienced before.

'Now we must leave this place quickly, I'm afraid Dan is in desperate need of help, deep in his mind something is broken. We need to get him to the Healer and that means we must travel out into Borderlands, a place very few of us travel to and fewer return from, but that is where we'll find help, I think. I've looked into what we of the ancient ways would call his soul, and there's restlessness beyond reach. Formless. Malignant. Growing. A link has been forged between whatever these creatures are and our lad Dan. A poison is spreading, the likes of which ordinary medicine can't reach.'

Frumentus went across to Dan, who was standing passively by the inert Turiel.

'What about the little creature; do we take it, leave it or kill it?'

'Dan's linked to it in a way I can't reach so I think we have to take it. Anyway killing's never the answer, Frumentus. Who knows what a little kindness might do to unlock what secrets it has to share. Let's ask Dan to carry it as he's clearly got a soft spot for it.'

As Hanok spoke, Dan seemed to come to life. 'Yes I'll willingly help Turiel, that's his name, I don't think he was trying to harm me, but help me.'

Turiel looked at Dan with mute gratitude. 'Turiel needs to get away. We's failed and will be hurt now because Dan's gone. Turiel's scared, they're so cruel, nasty, nasty things. Turiel's sorry that he hurt, biting and scratching, but he didn't know you were friends of Dan. We's can show you away out of this place.'

Dan was returning to vigorous life. Hanok had gone into one of his distant gazes. Turiel looked pleadingly. Frumentus decided. He opened his mouth as the pounding of the door recommenced with greater effect as the door began to buckle.

'Now, let's go now!' The party sprang to life, Frumentus carrying the writings, Hanok the cosh, and Dan, Turiel.

'Not this way!' cried Turiel, 'over there. Look over there. Go that way!' Swerving as he ran with Turiel held tightly, Dan altered course, outstripping the others he raced towards the gloomy unexplored end of the room. His swift progress was halted as he found himself in a corner, the others almost knocking him over as they reached the same dead end.

'Trapped!' Frumentus gasped, 'tricked!' He looked murderously at Turiel, who was still tucked under Dan's arm. 'You've betrayed us.' He moved towards Dan menacingly.

'No! Don't be a fool! He's trying to help us, I'm sure he is!' Dan shielded Turiel from Frumentus's advance. 'Quickly, where now, Turiel, they're almost through the door, we can't hide here.' Dan's trust in the goodness of Turiel seemed unnatural.

'We've no hope of getting to the passageway, look, the door's given way!' Frumentus's hand shook as he pointed to the far end of the room, where with a final screeching cry the door fell.

Turiel slipped from Dan's grasp. ''Here, we's go through here.' Reaching down, he quickly cleared away the accumulated dust and mess to reveal a large pull ring set within the floor.

Grasping it, Turiel began to lift the trap door the ring was attached to. Other hands eagerly joined the effort and soon steps leading down into the darkness were revealed. Without hesitation Turiel disappeared down into the gloom, with the others swiftly following behind. Hanok glanced back as he descended the steps, pulling the door closed behind him, and saw what looked like deep shadows alive with menace coming through the doorway. Feeling around the inside of the trapdoor he grunted with satisfaction. 'As I thought; manual override, the old ways are the best ways,' he muttered, as he slid home the bolt then turned to catch up with the others.

20

Early morning light gave the harshest of crags a softness, bathed as they were by its red golden glow. Creatures of the night retreated to the darker places, away from its revealing presence, as others stirred, unfolding into the day as its warmth seeped into their consciousness. This was a truly beautiful time in the Borderlands, and Zenobia loved to stand in gratitude for the gift of another day.

As a child she had been caught up in the wonder of the heavens. How was it that there should be such order and regularity in life? What caused the sun to rise and pass through the sky in regal progress towards lands beyond sight? How did the moon and stars maintain their stations in the sky with regularity, moving through its houses with the grace of a dancer? Why was it that human beings seemed to be the only creatures capable of rejoicing in the wonder of creation and in turn with their artistry mimic some beautiful thing with fine strokes of the brush, moulding of material or sensory formulation of words?

Her father had smiled in love as questions poured out of the enquiring mind. 'Always questions, never enough answers to satisfy that curiosity of yours, eh, my sweet thing? Some say all that we see is chance happening, a cosmic collision endlessly repeated until finally everything was just so and along came us, highly evolved from apes, ready to enjoy life to the full. Others say no there's more to life than we can see, there is in fact a mind behind all this that made it all be just so in order that we can enjoy life to the full. It's really a question, I think, of which came first, the mind or the matter. Did the mind evolve from the matter or did the matter, the building blocks of life as they call it, come from a mind; of course if you don't mind not knowing the answer – it doesn't matter!'

He chuckled, eyes twinkling. Zenobia did mind and she wanted answers to many things in life that were a puzzle.

Had time allowed and circumstances been different, her father would have taken his very inquisitive daughter to the Tewahedo, who were the keepers of the sacred writings and said to be skilled seekers in the arts of union between the physical and the divine. Both mother and father knew there was something special about their child, and family and friends were equally certain she was moon-kissed, blessed and gifted in life. Zenobia had heard her father speak of the Tewahedo, she knew they dwelt somewhere far south of home, a long and difficult journey away to the land known as Cush; someday he'd take there but that day never came.

Zenobia, a young girl, lost and alone in a world hostile to her kind, chose a different path and travelled south seeking to complete the journey her father dreamed of. It was a ruinous road less travelled and she was a vulnerable, beautiful child. With tragic inevitability, she fell into the hands of men who trafficked and traded her body down the length of the southern road. The child was lost back in the firestorm with her parents and so could not be reached by the ways of men. Zenobia became immune to their devices and desires, unflinching as their lust spilled into her. During those times, coldness, solid like a physical presence, formed deep within her that, glacier-like, carved depths within her being that waited to be filled at its passing. Eventually, Zenobia emerged like one awakening from a nightmare, fleeing the cruellest of keepers after emasculating his sleeping form.

She had been carried a long way south in the years following the destruction of her home, and her flight to freedom proved a simple journey along ancient trade routes, in the company of people who sensed that the young woman who asked to travel with them was a special one.

It was here that she gained her strength as the Tewahedo tended to her broken body and enquiring mind. Such was her thirst for knowledge, and her ability to grasp the reality of life beyond life, that the Tewahedo eventually decided that they must retrace Zenobia's journey, to bring her to the Great Heights close to the land where her parents had sought to resettle, for they knew the source of the knowledge of life was to be found there.

~ ~ ~

Spiro awoke to the sight of Zenobia framed in the entrance of the cave, the strengthening sunlight revealing her curvaceous form through the cotton undergown. He smiled broadly as he stretched his massive limbs to ease the cramps of the night's sleeping on the cave floor. 'You're a very pleasing sight for a man to awake to, I wish we could do this more often. Did you sleep well?' Stepping back into the cave, away from the sunshine, Zenobia smiled shyly. 'I love the morning light; the shadows of the night are dispelled at its coming and even the harshest things are softened as it touches them.'

'And how about you, Zenobia, are the shadows dispelled from within you? I felt the healing come into the cave last night, I hope it reached into the desolate places of your heart.'

'There are fewer shadows today. The healing came and reached to me, I did welcome it, invited it in and it dwelt with me. I can never forget what happened but the root of bitterness is withering.'

She smiled at Spiro and turned swiftly away from him, firmly resisting the longing her body felt for his embrace. She dressed swiftly, nose wrinkling at the smell of her clothing. 'I can't wait to return to Great Heights and be clean again, even if it's just for a while.' Smiling, she turned her attention to her horse with a handful of grain proffered on an outstretched hand. 'What do you think, home for a rest and a good clean stable with fresh water and food?' She blew gently onto the muzzle and reached up to scratch the twitching ears before laying her face against its flank. Now, working a brush along his back, she called across to Spiro, who had risen and was busily sorting out his over-tunic and belt from which hung a variety of weapons.

'Has our trooper survived the night, Spiro? I've not heard a sound from him so far.' Spiro crossed to the crude bed that had been created for the patient who lay still beneath the covers.

'Sergeant Dromas,' Spiro called, reading the identity tag, 'we've a sergeant for a patient and he seems to be alive. Don't think I want to salute him though; shall we call him Dromas? His wound looks clean, and there's no smell of death or decay hanging around him. You did a fine job with him considering what a mess he was yesterday.'

Having attended to the horse, Zenobia joined Spiro in appraising the state of the sergeant. 'I suspect the healing that came upon me last night has also touched our sergeant; he looks well enough to risk travelling. Shall we see if we can rouse him with the smell of your wonderful cooking? I'm famished and you're always ready to eat, let's hope he is too.'

Grinning, Spiro set to work on a cooking fire and a brace of freshly caught rabbits. Delighted at the surprised look on Zenobia's face, Spiro rumbled, 'whilst you were sleeping I thought I'd see what was around to eat, all this fighting makes you hungry, Zenobia, I've always said I'm quite the catch, nothing is too hard for me.'

Soon the meat was turning on a spit whilst vegetables sourced during the same nocturnal expedition simmered in the pot. Before long the savoury smell of roasting meat filled the cave and awakened an appetite in the sergeant, who groaned as he tried to move from his bed.

'Easy now, soldier,' Spiro called, 'you're safe with us, we've got that rock out of you, and the good news is nothing vital was damaged. You're going to be in a world of pain for a while, but you'll heal well enough. Here, try a little water; the food will be along shortly.' With surprising gentleness, the giant hands of Spiro held Dromas's head forward, sufficient for him to take some sips from the proffered cup.

'My Zenobia, she's a trusting soul, she'd rather take people at their word. Me, I'm not so good, I need to look a man in the eyes to see if he speaks truly. I don't trust anyone easily, so convince me that you choose to help us.'

Dromas knew there was no going back, in one day his life had changed for ever. 'I'm going to follow her, you have my word.'

Zenobia crossed to where Dromas was now struggling to sit up. 'Go slowly now, let me help you.' Her arm slid behind his shoulders and together they achieved a more upright position on the bed. 'Spiro is a marvel with food, quite delicious dishes come like rabbits out of a hat, in this case literally.'

Smiling, she checked over his battered torso, marvelling at how swiftly the flesh was mending. 'I'm sorry but we are going to have to try to move you today, it won't be safe to stay here with all that's gone on.' Zenobia flushed slightly at what that phrase implied.

'Death is a terrible thing and to bring death haunts me, I'm sorry for those that were lost out there, they were just children really, serving a soulless beast intent only in preserving itself at any cost. If you follow me, Dromas, it will be into a conflict with the beast. Other troopers will die, maybe we will die. If we do, it will be for an honourable cause.'

'I don't want to die for nothing, Zenobia, if I go back it will be terrible for me, you are my hope of life, and I will follow you into whatever the future may bring.'

Before an hour had elapsed a crude litter was attached to the saddle and Dromas was being dragged along the poles, carried when the terrain became too rocky. The journey was slow and painful, but having traversed the eastern base of the mountain the party set their course for the distant range that towered over the plain.

The Great Heights were currently recognised as the boundary of the Citadel's interest, and nestling in those heights lay safety. With shadows lengthening after a hard day's journey the three stopped to shelter in their coolness, to await the moonrise to guide their onward travels.

Above the vast plain the Citadel floated immune, immutable, a hated enemy to those who dwelt on the Great Heights. To Dromas it represented a brutal past life where shameful things were done to squatters to cleanse the land, as the world averted its gaze. Land clearances prepared the way for the ascent of a people who would live in the sky, a people who held the secrets to endless life.

Spiro was also gazing in the direction of the cube but his attention was drawn to something far smaller.

'I think we're going to be having company quite soon. Zenobia, be ready to fight, for we're surely too slow to avoid them.'

21

In furious rage, Samyaza led the charge, bursting through the door that gave one last groan before swinging drunkenly open on twisted hinges. The others poured in behind him, seeking the enemy within. They howled in impotent protest into the empty chamber, oblivious to the trap door lid silently closing in the darkened corner. 'It's all lost, the boy, the book, the cripple. He came and took them from us while we've been abroad amongst them!' Zarak spat the words. 'Damn and curse them.

They spread through the chamber and soon came to the trapdoor but found it to be unyielding, as the bolt beneath was extremely thick. Frustration deepened as attempts made to smash through the door proved equally futile. 'It's like someone has put a charm on the thing!'

Zarak threw himself onto the floor in disgust, his unspoken thoughts accessible to all. 'Surely they're lost to us. All the furies will come for us as soon as it is known where we are. All we've patiently worked towards over these years will be quenched.'

Samyaza drew very close to Zarak as he grasped him by the throat and squeezed. 'Be very careful what you think, Zarak, we wouldn't want the others to catch the fear that seems to have infected you. Your panic is unsettling and unnecessary. The Nephilim will rise. The boy has the potential to become what lies within him.

We must do more to aid his awakening by bringing down the Citadel and forcing conflict. The hunters can go after these people once they've deposited Marcus at the home.'

Samyaza stared down the sullen faces of Watchers who preferred the shadows, none could hold his gaze. He continued with icy menace. 'Irreversible forces once unleashed will bring chaos that far exceeds the deluge those aeons ago. We shall have our Armageddon, we shall have our revenge on Him and we shall see the Nephilim rise to take their rightful place. Lords of the earth!'

22

Through the heat haze Zenobia saw them, stragglers bathed in dust, unaware that they were not alone in the vastness of the wilderness. From their demeanour, she decided that they were more troubled by what lay behind them than any threats ahead. In the gloom she counted three people struggling to make headway in clothing and footwear unsuited for the punishing conditions of the Borderlands. One, taller and more striking than the rest of the group, appeared to be carrying a child on his shoulders. Stepping out of dark shadow, she boldly approached them.

'I kill people from your Citadel! Why should I not kill you?'

'My lady, please! We mean no harm, we are fleeing great peril and our friend needs a deep healing, something grows within his mind. We have passed through some extraordinary days that I can speak of, but please, the blade.'

Zenobia lowered the blade and listened as their story unfolded. The spokesman for the group had the demeanour of a leader dressed in comfortable jacket and trousers, and he spoke with clear authority and integrity. The one dressed in a sweat-stained grimy uniform looked ill at ease, shifting from foot to foot, anxiously looking behind himself from time to time as they spoke. The tallest had a striking appearance that would, Zenobia decided, have been attractive had it not been for the unwaveringly vacant stare. On his shoulders was one who had the stature of a frail child but the face of an old man with near translucent skin and what appeared to be crippled feet. Emerging from beneath his dark hooded robe, his bony hand softly stroked the young man's hair, whilst the thin lips ceaselessly moved as if comforting the boy.

She drew close to Dan and looked steadily into his eyes. The gloom could not obscure a strange shadow that lay within the boy. If anything, it seemed to reach out to Zenobia as a kindred spirit. She drew back, convinced of the truth of the strangers' tale, choosing to trust.

Decision made, she turned and called into the darkness. 'I think this will go down in our memories as quite the most unusual of days don't you think, Spiro?'

'I think it will indeed, Zenobia, I think it will indeed,' chuckled Spiro, emerging from the darkness sheathing his knife, causing Frumentus to cry out in surprise. 'I'm guessing you're not wanting them killed just yet.'

'No, not yet and probably not at all, we'll go together. Some very strange things are afoot and it seems our lives are to become intertwined.'

Zenobia smiled as she spoke. 'This is my world, gentlemen; you have come from another world that has destroyed much, and as you rightly feared there are many who would wish you harm. I do not wish this for you, and you travel under my protection, and the protection of Zenobia is no small thing.'

23

Shylock hurried back towards Hanok's library, intent now on retracing his steps in his pursuit of Marcus. He reasoned that the most efficient way to find him was by tracing the abductors of Dan. Deputy Director Davidson had outlined the options available to secure the Citadel, largely based on Shylock's assessment of risk. Eventually the Convocation had agreed to a proactive course of action that could have the Citadel lowered to earth. With Shylock's help Davidson had answered what questions he could about the disappearance of Dan and the actions of Frumentus and Hanok in pursuing the abductors.

Now teams of engineers supported by repair bots were at work on the ground and within the structure, preparing for a smooth descent for what was to be described to the population as essential maintenance. This would be the opportunity Shylock needed to get through the acoustic drive chamber as they powered down easing the structure into the waiting arms of the landing cradle.

Shylock attempted to increase his pace but found that his own energy levels were depleting. Synths were primarily designed to function within the Citadel they recharged constantly. The further from this energy source they travelled, the weaker the replenishment became and reliance on stored power was triggered, causing power-saving functions to kick in. Passing close to the acoustic drivers had inevitably led to some system damage, all of which meant Shylock was slowing down just when he needed to speed up.

Undeterred, he pressed on, passing through the maze of tunnels. Eventually he detected the presence of those he sought.

Shylock filed a status report of his discoveries to Davidson which would, as with all synth activity, be uploaded whenever he was next in the Citadel. Marcus lived and Shylock was following.

Before long the pathway diverged; the host were heading toward the descending Citadel whereas Marcus's trail led towards the Borderlands. Shylock updated his findings then turned to follow the pathway Marcus and two other humans now travelled.

As he hurried on, Shylock considered the likely identity of the additional humans; he considered the probability of their being allies of the Citadel, rescuers of Marcus, as low. Marcus was in the hands of enemies of the Citadel who were to use him for ransom or as a bargaining chip. This suggested that there was a combined force behind the attacks. An ancient enemy and an alien force, the former fanatically intent on the utter annihilation of the city state, a futile ambition. Could the latter form a new alliance and prove a deadlier threat? The risk analysis would need to be swiftly recalculated and the threat status upgraded to imminent and severe.

Shylock reported these new concerns to Davidson and this time requested that support vehicles be sent in the likely direction of his travel. He hoped that they could find him and provide an energy boost and ground support against these hostiles. The report was queued to send when the interference cleared.

Emerging from the tunnels, traces of Marcus dispersed, windblown in the vastness that was the Borderlands. Shylock found himself unable to compute a direction of travel with any degree of certainty, as he was reaching the edge of his safe operating-limit. There grew in him a renewed sense of his own frailty, a feature

Marcus had programmed into Shylock to create something more than synth. Something almost human that would owe a filial loyalty towards its creator. During that process an ancient mantra for justice had been programmed to loop continuously in the recesses of Shylock's processors. *'I am a synth. Has not a synth eyes? Has not a synth hands, dimensions, senses... If a human wrongs a synth, what should his punishment be by human example? Why, revenge!'*

As Shylock stood facing the uncertainty of the Borderlands, the self-awareness running in the background programming arose, no longer entirely suppressed as his power supply ebbed away. Fearfully he cried out with increasing desperation for his father who he was so driven to find. 'Marcus! Where do I find you, which way do I go?' His repeated calling was swept away by the wind into the easterly lands from where came no reply.

24

The journey across the Borderlands was slow. Dromas's bruised and battered body jarred over the rock-strewn landscape, giving rise to a near continual groaning, which in turn added to the burning, parched rawness of his throat. The group extended in a line, with Spiro leading the horse, followed by Frumentus and then Dan carrying Turiel. At the rear of the party Hanok and Zenobia walked together. Hanok carrying the writings in a pannier taken from Zenobia's horse, the leather painfully rubbing on his thin shoulders. Zenobia was eager to question and probe for the weaknesses of the Citadel but did so cautiously so as not to stifle the freely speaking man.

'Tell me, Hanok. That which you carry is a heavy looking burden, it must be of great value for you to struggle to bear its weight day by day.'

Hanok acknowledged the question with a grunt and nod of the head. 'It is, my lady, a heavy burden but as to its value or its meaning I cannot say. It was the only other thing taken when Dan was snatched, and so evidently it has value to them. I keep it because I am searching for something, a secret held within the Corporation.'

Zenobia's smile faded and she stilled herself, as a dust devil swirled at her feet and the scent of the parched earth filled the air. Very quietly she asked to know more, and then waited in silence as

Hanok wrestled with his desire to tell and the caution that prevented him from trusting anyone who was an enemy of his people. The indecision passed across his weathered features, wind-scorched from wandering the Borderlands in search of answers. Eventually he allowed himself to trust, and out of his heart poured forth the failures of the Corporation.

'We have to hide our weakness well for we are hated and hunted, our memories of past pain lead us to inflict pain to protect ourselves.' He looked appraisingly at Zenobia, who stood wide-eyed at the news of vulnerability.

'I imagine that includes you.'

Her family had believed in the words of a pacifist preacher who encouraged them to go live again on the land of their fathers. '*Build sanctuaries, trust in the goodness of God to protect you and pierce their oppressors' hearts with the justice of our cause.*' No! The firestorm had come, and all was gone.

She turned and walked away from Hanok, flushed in her anger.

'My lady, please don't despise me. I don't seek endless life. My quest was for the truth!'

Truth had led him struggling to reach desolate places buried deep in the uninhabited zones. At times despairing of life he had pressed on, by machine whose sensors scanned for any signs of life and when that failed, on foot, until he found it. The single-storey building that held scores of the aged, dying slow lonely deaths, lost with fragile broken minds and weakened bodies. An endlessly slow slide into the misery and regret of a life lived alone.

'I found the truth that life is not endless, our people die. That can't be all there is, Zenobia, there had to be more to life than death.' The Citadel drove him to the desert places and in turn they returned Hanok to the Citadel.

Well he remembered his quest for ancient wisdom that spoke of such things, a wisdom held in safe keeping until the fire.

'Somewhere I've read of a life that is eternal, not endless. My memory fails but it could be that this is the book that will give me the answers I seek. Why else would it be the one book stolen? That is my quest, to discover this life and offer it to all in need but especially those in the homes.'

Zenobia felt a clutch at her heart, a flicker no more, calling her to trust Hanok's words. She pushed such feelings away.

'I doubt that if ever you found this life, you would you share its secret with others. Look at the record of your people! They love the power that control of life brings!'

Hanok stood with his hands by his side, defenceless, 'You know you can easily take this book from me, I am just a tired old man. But think. Have these strange circumstances brought your world and mine together to find the way to a new life?'

A dark desire to destroy the writings compelled Zenobia forward before her instinct for survival kicked in. Grabbing Hanok, she threw him to the ground as the flash of a laser bolt shot past his face.

25

'Shoot the old one on the left.'

'On the left?'

'That's right, the one on the left.'

'Did you say right?'

'No, left! The old one on the left, the one on the right isn't old and isn't on the left, is he!?'

'No, it's a she. I'll shoot the one on the left and clip the one on the right. That'll bring the others back from over the hill then we'll have 'em except the blondie, he's got to go back to the fella with the cloak in the tunnel, the weirdo, oh and let's not forget the package, he wanted a package as well.'

Taking careful aim, the hunter fired.

'You missed the one on the left and the one on the right.'

'I know I did but they moved, didn't they. The one on the right chucked the one on the left out of the way as I fired.'

'Next time I'll shoot and you can spot,' hissed the first hunter, peering out into the haze.

'Why, it's my rifle, get your own if you want to shoot.'

'It's not that I want to shoot, it's that I want to hit what I shoot at!'

The argument quietly rolled on between the pair as they waited in anticipation for their quarry to break cover.

'I can't see a thing from here, are they still there?'

'Must be, where else can they go, it's just flat out there.'

In fact, it wasn't. Zenobia had thrown Hanok into a shallow gulley where he lay dazed. Meanwhile she was working her way around towards the back of the two assailants with lithe serpentine movements, flat to the ground. At that moment, appearing over the crest of the hill, the rest of the party minus Dromas emerged warily, having been alerted by the fizz of a laser rifle being discharged.

'Look, there are the rest of them. Don't shoot the one on the right, that's Blondie, we needs him alive. Have a go at another.'

'Blondie looks a bit weird, don't he? What's that on his head, a dwarf?'

'No idea, our man mentioned nothing about his headwear or a dwarf, why not knock that off and then get the fat fella in the uniform or better still the giant.'

With an effective range of over a mile, the rifle was the weapon of choice of hunters; albeit cumbersome to reload, it made up for this inadequacy by the fact that the pulse of energy stayed true. As he took careful aim the weapon kicked slightly and the pair watched with satisfaction as the pulse threw Turiel from Dan's shoulder. Blood and fangs flew as Turiel fell heavily and lay still.

The process of recharging underway, the two huddled out of view unaware of Dan, who seeing the smouldering body of Turiel charged with unknown ferocity towards the source of the pulse. He fell upon the unprepared hunters, tearing at flesh with bare hands and teeth. Within moments the fight was confused into a swirling cloud of dust with cries and shouts mixed with an animal roar.

'Stab him, cut him, gut him, come on!'

'No, he's the blondie, he's valuable! Knock him out, use the stun of the gun to calm the animal down.'

The flash of light emerging from the melee proved that experience triumphed over brute force, and with the dust settling the truth was revealed. Dan lay inert, whilst the hunters tentatively felt for injuries, gasping for breath following the brutal encounter.

'He bit me, 'e's cut you. Did you see him move; no wonder they want him, with training he'll be quite the one to watch.'

'Come on, let's get the rest and get out of here, look, get the one on the left.'

Somewhat blinded by the sunshine, Frumentus peered hopefully forward; he was alone.

'Down, you fool.' The call came from nowhere but Frumentus dropped like a stone, avoiding the laser pulse aimed at his heart.

'Stay low, keep still.' The command was clear and Frumentus willingly obeyed.

Chambering another charge, the hunter readied for a killing shot.

'Have a look, is he there still or has he gone?'

'He's gone to ground. Now we're stuffed. We've got Blondie and they've got us surrounded. Let's parlay.'

Standing up, the first hunter called out. 'We're only after Blondie here, that's all they want. If you want to live past today, walk away, we'll take him with us. We're supposed to kill you and we've the weapons to do that but we won't if you agree to our parlay. What do you say?'

Standing in the swirling dust kicked up by the strengthening wind, the hunter was unable to hear the whirring sound of a strongly thrown blade that sliced through the atmosphere and implanted itself in his chest. Slumping slowly forward onto his knees, and then head-first into the ground, he fell without a cry.

His companion froze. Emerging from the dust cloud with death in her cold black eyes stepped Zenobia. So fearfully intense was the stare that the hunter's dark soul was paralysed, a ready victim for her wrath.

His end would have been swift had not the voice of Hanok called from the bleakness. 'No. I would know whence he came and to whom this creature answers!' It was enough of a commanding presence to forestall the hand of Zenobia and quell the anger of Spiro, who came wraithlike out of the gloom to reclaim his thrown knife.

Death was deferred, not denied; the hunter knelt before his captors reluctant at first to speak, however pain persuaded him to tell his tales and when all was said and done his neck was snapped.

Now they knew both Dan and the writings were of value to the shadowy creatures, who in turn could engage low grade mercenaries to carry out their wishes. More than knowledge, they gained transport as the hunters had a Landy, used to transport unfortunates to the homes. Their intervention became a vindication of Hanok's words.

'Very well, Hanok, it seems you have a tale to tell that others don't want to be told. I will speak for you when we reach the Great Heights.'

Hanok looked down at the corpses, shocked by the violence of events and the news that the cloaked ones were determined to recover both the boy and the book. Zenobia knelt by the unconscious Dan, carefully examining the effect of the stun that had scorched his temple.

'Stunning at this range can be as fatal as the kill shot, but he lives. When he wakes, his head will feel itself on fire and he may not be able to see or hear too clearly, but healing will come.'

Frumentus staggered forward, the limp form of Turiel in his arms.

'Shot clean off his shoulders. Dan will be devastated when he comes round. His attack reminded me of how Turiel fought us back in the chamber, all tearing and biting in a tremendous fury, it was almost like Dan was Turiel.'

At his words, Hanok came out of his daze. 'You may well have it just right, Frumentus, you clever fellow! I think it may be that those creatures want Dan back because there's something of them in him.

When I looked for his soul, there seemed to be an ice gradually forming within him, freezing his life in order that another could grow. Turiel has been close to Dan all the time we've been travelling, speaking to him, what is to say that he's not continued the freezing of Dan's soul? I didn't see that before but now it was as if the two were becoming one. His whisperings encouraging the alien life within Dan to keep growing.'

Zenobia stood, concern in her voice. 'We must get him to the Great Heights, into the healing place, soon, or I fear we will never be able save your friend from the growing ice within him. I asked you for the book before all this happened, will you give it to me now? There are those I know who may be able to interpret these strange times we are passing through.'

Removing the strapping that held the package to his back, Hanok gently placed the writings in the hand of Zenobia, who carefully held them, wondering why people would be sent to kill to get such things back.

'Spiro, bring Dromas to the Landy, he can tell us how the vehicle works. Frumentus, you are going to learn to drive. Strip the hunters of anything useful and release my horse to find his way home.'

Zenobia's energy brought the whole party to life and in short order they were ready to travel. Dromas was painfully positioned next to Frumentus who was at the wheel of the vehicle. After a few juddering attempts that brought forth colourful language from Dromas, the Landy began to make some smoother progress, climbing up a gentle incline that marked the tentative beginning of a climb out of the Border lands towards the Great Heights.

Seated in the back, Hanok gasped in wonder as he turned to view the journey across that arid, inhospitable place. It wasn't the sight of barren land that caught his breath however, but that of the vast citadel in graceful descent towards the earth. As Hanok stared out across the plain, words long forgotten came to his mind and were on his lips almost simultaneously; '*And on the pedestal these words appear: 'My name is Ozymandias, king of kings: Look on my works, ye Mighty, and despair!'*

Zenobia, turning at the sound, looked on incredulously; 'I have dreamt of such a day as this when it would fall, but never did I think I would see it. What strange days these are, what do they mean, I wonder?' As she spoke, the sound of powerful motors and moving metal long dormant were heard across the land as the arms of the cradles slowly opened, preparing to offer a welcoming embrace to the descending structure. Other words rose up to the forefront of Hanok's mind: *"How the mighty have fallen, and the weapons of war perished!"*

26

The remainder of the journey to the Great Heights proved uneventful. By the end of their drive, Frumentus had mastered control of the vehicle and they found themselves at the foot of the towering cliff-face. Spiro was clear about the method of ascent. 'The journey up can just about be made in the vehicle, do you see that track there?' Spiro thick fingers traced the outline of a sharply winding track that led up the mountain. 'There will be places where we will need to get out and push the Landy, and for the last leg we will have to carry Dromas and Dan. The sooner we start, the sooner we will get up there.'

Eventually, after much effort, they crested the top and stepped out onto the heights. Behind them a panoramic view was laid out, dominated by the Citadel now nearing completion of its descent. Many had gathered to see for themselves the truth of the impossible news that had flown by word of mouth throughout the region.

As Zenobia came into view, a gale of cheering erupted from the crowd and her name was chanted back and forth, her victory before their eyes. The acclaim grew louder as the crowd pressed ever closer, now strewing her way with foliage from the trees; they knew where she was heading, and they loved her for it.

Walking behind her, Hanok and Frumentus could not fail to wonder at the status of the woman so evidently beloved by these people. Never had they experienced such unrestrained joy directed at another person, or seen the trust and hope placed in them.

The concept of an infallible leader didn't seem to occur to them. In their naivety they loved her. *Very odd but quite touching,* thought Hanok, ignoring as best he could any of the more hostile words and gestures directed towards him and fellow citizens of the Citadel as they trailed behind the returning heroine.

Spiro was busy supervising the transport of Dan and Dromas. They were to be taken directly to the healing place for attention, and once his mission was accomplished he fully intended to catch up with his squad in the hopes they had left him something to drink in toast of their successful raid.

As he followed Zenobia's path Frumentus wondered at the sight of so many children playing and laughing in the warm sunshine. It was such an unusual sight to the man from the Citadel, and stirred within him sadness. He saw the hushed corridors and quiet rooms; the muted hum of the acoustic drivers was a stark contrast to the joyful exuberance of the young. Such sights and sounds were lost to his kind.

It was harvest-time, and Hanok marvelled at the fruitfulness of the land, its fertility due in part to the heavy rainfall that swept in from the west, partly from the volcanic heritage but mostly due to the industry of the people.

Life abounded, the purples of fresh picked grapes and golden hue of the late wheat harvest, and scents of fresh flowers combined with the aroma of freshly turned rich earth to become a wonderful assault on his senses. Food grew everywhere, trees, bushes, planted crops bursting with abundance. Young and old, no longer curious about the sights of the Citadel, worked easily together to claim the bounteous supply. The sounds of music and song filled the air as the three walked.

Frumentus pondered Zenobia's explanation of the fertility all around. 'We work with the land, Frumentus, we honour it as stewards of the good gifts, giving back when we take so it can be passed on more fertile to our children's children.' Here, the hope was for the future generations, in the Citadel, with those alive now, endlessly extending their time.

'Is no one troubled by the thought that passing on to the next generation means you're passing away in this one, do you not fear death?'

Zenobia stopped walking to allow Frumentus to catch up with her. 'Frumentus, to die young is an injustice, to live under tyranny without hope and beauty is our tragedy. To die full of years holds no fear. There is more to life than death. We live here in exile, for you have taken our once-fertile land and made it barren, but we have hope that the better life is yet to come. For now, we have made this barren place fertile.'

A herd of sheep and goats drifted past them following the tune of the shepherd boy as he sang a simple song. *'Follow me, come follow me, follow me and you will see: refreshment for your soul; and a body remade whole. Come and see, come follow me. To new pastures we will go.'* The flock trotted behind their shepherd, trusting his leading to rich new pastures, leaving Frumentus to watch and wonder at the messages of life all around.

Zenobia smiled. 'Come on, Frumentus, we're nearly there now, if these sights are surprising to you, I think you will enjoy what I have to show you.'

She set off again with a lightness of step on the path that followed the cliff-edge, eventually disappearing over the side into a natural crater on the far side of which was a substantial walled complex which appeared to have been cut from the red rock itself. The sheer outer walls rose fantastically high, disappearing into the mountain whilst a single circular gateway offered access into the complex.

As they approached, the gate swung open and three figures robed in white stepped into the sun. Their effect on those in the crowd who were following Zenobia's progress was instant, the jubilant cries dying on their lips, their motion stopping as if held back by the presence of the three. Hanok and Frumentus were reluctant to continue following Zenobia. They were awed by the presence of the figures, but fearing to be left amongst the crowd they cautiously continued.

Zenobia reached the three. She bowed deeply to each one before reaching for their hands, and, taking each into her own, she kissed them before rising to speak. She turned and beckoned Hanok and Frumentus forward, and as she did so the three turned and walked back through the gateway into the complex. The crowds once again raised their voices to the heavens; their cries went with Zenobia, Hanok and Frumentus as they followed the three inside.

Beyond the walls, Hanok was amazed to find gardens of scented beauty and subtle sounds everywhere, the sound of water running, splashing, trickling over pebbles, gushing over cascades whilst springs bubbled joyfully from the ground. Trees were in abundance, some laden with fruit, others providing dappled shade, forming miniature parklands and squares where lush grass lay immaculately tended. Finely carved seats and ornate gazebos were artfully placed to gain the maximum enjoyment from the splendid assault on the senses. Many winding pathways, some of gravel, others of stone, weaved intriguingly into the lush vegetation, inviting exploration.

The central pathway, however, led onwards in a near straight course towards a domed building of considerable height. This was constructed of bright white stone and adorned with many windows, and with broad steps leading up to the entrance portico and a highly polished honey brown door.

'What is this beautiful place?' Frumentus asked in blissful wonder, 'I've never experienced feelings like this in all the chemical wonder we've created. It is like another world, a place of peace and pleasure where time stands still.'

Smiling, Zenobia was herself gladdened as always by the nourishing effect the garden had on Frumentus. 'This is the pleasure garden. It's a waiting place, it's good to come here – it's just so very hard to leave.'

'Why would you ever want to leave? To return to the dust and the mess, I think not!'

'Frumentus, there are times when we have to leave what is perfect to work amongst the imperfect suffering and sorrow. Now I must leave you both and speak with the Tewahedo, as may you. Your friend Dan will soon reach the healing place, and once I have finished my time here I will go to him and see what can be done. Hanok, I would speak with you a moment more if I may. Farewell for now, Frumentus, I hope to see you soon.'

Walking alone with Hanok, Zenobia gently quizzed the frail man. 'Hanok, what does it mean that the Citadel has descended, is it part of the purposes you spoke of earlier, does it mean that your news of the failure of endless life is more widely known?'

'My lady, I do not know why such a thing has happened, although it was always planned for, this is the first time the Citadel has returned to the earth. Something of vast importance lies behind this and I suspect it is an internal threat to the whole complex. It would be a mistake to think we are helpless at this time; if you were to choose this time to destroy us, a greater destruction than can be imagined would be unleashed. We have strong allies in the west who need us, or rather need what only we can supply. They would swiftly come to our aid and brutally defend our cause.'

Zenobia turned to go, quickly walking towards the building. On the top of the steps she turned. 'Thank you, Hanok, in this place only the truth can be spoken. I know of the brutality of which you speak. It would be terrible for our people if that was to come again.'

Turning away from him, she entered into a small antechamber where the steam from a bubbling bath enveloped her in its welcoming embrace. Naked, she lowered herself into the bubbles with a sigh of deep pleasure and allowed her mind to wander where it would, unafraid of the places it might go.

27

Hanok soon caught up with Frumentus who was strolling in a leisurely manner through grounds, frequently stopping to admire the handiwork of the gardeners. 'We have nothing like this, do we, Hanok? In our world we've nothing that grows or gives pleasure like this. Are we not the more sophisticated culture? We float the Citadel in the sky but when you come to this place beyond the Borderlands you discover new wonders. I can't help but think our people are missing out on the possibility of having this life for themselves. If they knew what colours and scents and sights lay beyond the Citadel perhaps they would be disquieted with their life and seek this one.'

Hanok kept in step with Frumentus, listening to the rich deep tones in his animated voice. A change was coming over his companion; it was as if colour was entering into a picture that previously had been black and white.

'You know, Frumentus, I think if you went home with news of this place the people would not believe you. Their minds have been filled with the stories the Corporation tells them. In the Citadel they are safe, life is fulfilled and endless, labour and toil are virtually unheard of, and minds are satisfied with a reality that's virtual. How would you describe the scent of one of these flowers, the taste of that spring water or the sense of well-being you have when you're here? You see, you can't explain things, our people back home have no capacity to comprehend.'

Frumentus's heart grew heavy as Hanok spoke; he knew the reality of his words and felt a sorrow that here was goodness that others would deny themselves as they were incapable of comprehending its existence. He could understand why if you looked out from the Citadel the vista was of the threatening and arid Borderlands wherein lay the enemy.

'Frumentus, you can't explain this to people, but you can show it to them. I don't particularly mean record it to show them, for who trusts what they see on the screens these day? Just more alternative reality, your truth not mine. No, I don't mean that and I doubt they would willingly travel even if they were able to. What I mean is that you can take some of this back with you, not the physical stuff but the change it is evidently bringing over you just being here. Your very life would be a witness to what you have experienced of far greater power than mere words or pictures.'

Hanok smiled warmly as Frumentus absorbed his words, and his entire countenance lifted as his posture seemed to grow taller and straighter.

'Thank you, Hanok, I do feel I am changing, growing almost, like one of these plants, it's a wonderful sensation of growing into something new and away from what I was before, a sort of unfolding.' He saw again the spurned child, criticized and chided for every errant action and misspoken word who fell into muteness curled in on himself, frightened of failing, unlovable.

'It's strange here, Hanok, this place makes you see the truth of things. I've never trusted anyone to tell them about my life before but here, with you, it's fine. I can't ever remember being valued or commended or embraced. I know they call me 'the fool' now and for a time in my growing years I played at being the fool as it gave me a place to belong. Of course later as my future path was decided for me I truly earned the name with role of Head of Security. Then when I destroyed the writings that name of 'fool' echoed all the louder in my head. Now we've embarked on the wild journey, things have changed for me, and I am so glad that they have!'

They continued to walk and talk with an easy familiarity of a growing friendship. As they did so, Hanok felt ready to share his concerns over the Telemeric project and his journeys to the far-flung homes. 'I also have to say that I suspect Marcus was actually behind the destruction of the books, I know you say you entered the codes incorrectly in the drill, but what if you simply entered what you were told? Was it not Marcus who gave you the sequence? What if you entered what he said correctly? The code sequences are randomly selected from outside the complex and relayed to the control room for you to enter, isn't that right?'

Frumentus nodded mutely. 'There is in fact no requirement or expectation of anyone else being with you, it's not part of the usual drill, is it? So why was Marcus there, why did he get the sequence? How do you know you got it wrong?'

'Because Marcus told me I did,' admitted Frumentus. 'I never thought to check back into the records that the actual numbers given matched the ones I entered. There was an enquiry. Marcus shielded me from it. Virtually the day after the fire, Shylock was with me everywhere I went. I was clearly instructed to keep away from the control room whilst things were looked into and somehow I never got to go back there.'

Hanok's suspicions gave Frumentus a different perspective on Marcus's actions. The destruction of the writings had caused a huge scandal, which was a terrible mistake; or could it have been a deliberate act? 'Why would Marcus deliberately destroy the library, would the risk of discovery end his career?'

Hanok stopped. 'I don't know exactly why but I suspect it is linked to the book that we recovered from the chamber, the one taken with Dan. Before the 'accident' I had, shall we say, "acquired without official recognition" quite a collection of the older books and papers for my library. The Convocation had allowed me to continue my investigation into the failings of endless life. My time wandering in the Borderlands had weakened me. I hoped a time of study through these writings might shed light on our human condition, the wisdom of the ages and all that, the point being that no one really kept an eye on me and I was allowed to do as I pleased. You yourself know that my library was a rather eccentric design and they allowed me to have my way. In time I was even allowed to remove the sensors. Everybody was happy that my concerns had been quietly dealt with and life in the Corporation would simply go on as before.

'I think when the incinerators were 'accidently' ignited in your drill, Marcus thought all books would be destroyed, especially our one. When it was discovered that this book and others existed, it was taken. How it was discovered I do not know, why it wasn't simply destroyed I can't say, but I would be willing to guess they are linked to Dan. From what we've encountered it would appear that the lad is of interest to those creatures, if they were closely watching him they would have discovered my little treasure trove existed.

'What they have not realised is that there is greater treasure yet in the library just waiting to be unearthed, I can recall it more easily here than there, it contains the pathway to this life, if ever you get the chance go and look for the library of sixty-six. You see, my friend, it could be that you were used by Marcus, and that he has used others, or is being used by them, to prevent us discovering what is written in the book. Why he would go to such lengths I do not know, but I assume it is connected to what I have witnessed hidden away in the homes, that endless life is not a gift we can continue to offer to the world.'

Subtle blues, flaming reds with a hosts of different hues, the flowers' scent filled the air with the aroma of honey and spice as the water trickled and danced and the leaves' made a musical accompaniment in the gentle breeze. Frumentus breathed them all in deeply and felt yet more fresh life flowing into his being. 'I wish we could stay here, Hanok, suspended in this moment in time, it is truly beautiful.'

Hanok sighed. 'It truly is, and to stay would be a pleasure; but to *know*, Frumentus, to know what those words mean drives me onwards. I believe for reasons I know not that in those words lie clues to another way of life, one that is eternal not endless, a life of a different quality altogether, in fact you know, Frumentus, as I look around and see the way you are coming alive, I'd say this is a good way to describe eternal life.

'I hope that our journey will lead us to those who can translate the writings we have with us, and perhaps even explain what it means to live life in harmonious communion, free from all suffering, sorrow and sadness. I also hope that the atmosphere of this place will seep into the heart of our young Dan, though I fear a force of life very different to this is at work within him.'

As the time passed the two walked and talked at ease with each other in the paradise they found themselves in. Eventually Zenobia came to them, dressed in a simple white tunic with a golden belt at her waist, her hair piled high on her head. Frumentus found himself quite intoxicated by her appearance; her eyes were striking with their dark beauty, lips containing a pleasing plumpness, her nose and ears a delight to the eye. Fine facial features were supported by an elegant neck, broad shoulders and sinewy arms no more than hinted at the steely strength he had witnessed in recent days. The suggestion of a cleavage and the swell of her breasts drew and held his attention, stirring him in ways previously unknown. She acknowledged his interest with a slight smile and dip of her head before turning to Hanok. 'I have been with the three and we have opened the book. Hanok, we can read it! The language is Ge'ez, it is the language of the Tewahedo. They would meet with you, Hanok, and speak of what they've read. Please come with me, both of you. Frumentus, you will bathe and rest. Hanok, you must be prepared to meet them, nothing unclean can enter this place so your preparations will be more extensive.'

28

Shylock remained unmoving, his cry echoing through the wilderness, he would not turn away from the search. Shylock's duty and desire was to report all the events of recent days to Marcus and to get him to a place of safety. If he had not survived the trauma then the task would change.

He travelled towards the docking site in the expectation of finding transportation. It seemed obvious that those who had kidnapped Marcus would be heading towards the Great Heights so he would commandeer fast transport in the name of Marcus and pursue.

As expected, there was great activity amongst the troopers with nearly the entire brigade deployed. Dust clouds swirled, the cradle arms yawned wide as the crescendo built from the descending Citadel. Landies worked hard, towing lengthy trailers laden with electrified fencing and land mines. High overhead vapour streams were evident, tracing out the reassuring message 'we are with you'.

The scale of the work was truly awesome as the descent of the vast cube dwarfed the surrounding land, and even then only one corner would actually touch down into the grasp of the docking cradle.

Shylock's authority enabled him to commandeer a hover jet and, within the hour he had mastered the machine and set off towards the Great Heights at speed. By the end of the day his journey had led him far out into the Borderlands; the machine carried extra reserves and Shylock himself was fully recharged. With night vision capability his was a ceaseless search. At all times his sensors were scanning the landscape in great sweeps seeking for any traces of life. Towards the middle of the night he was alerted to the presence of death.

As Shylock examined the clothing of the bloated part-eaten corpses he also detected traces of Marcus's fluids, hair and skin. These men had been near Marcus, probably carrying him. The traces were faint and suggested to Shylock that some time had passed since they were last in contact with him, which in turn led him to conclude that his first assessment was incorrect. It now appeared Marcus had been taken somewhere in the western sector of the Borderlands. Shylock headed west, following the tracks of vehicle for as long as they were evident, after which he began quartering the land for further evidence of life. Eventually traces of life led him to the home.

Upon entering the home, the first thing Shylock became aware of was the smell; stale urine enhanced by the unusually warm temperature. A bright corridor stretched away before him with doors on both sides of its length, terminating at what appeared to be a communal area. Guide-rails ran down each side of the walls, which had a bright yellow finish, whilst the floor was bare. Overhead the lights gave the place a stark clinical appearance. Shylock turned to the manager, who stood passively at his side, satisfied that Shylock had permission to be there.

'Tell me, what is this place used for?' Shylock's tone was that of a superior synth to a junior.

'The home is one of several established to receive certain parties from the Citadel. Here we can house one hundred and fifty, we are the latest and largest.' Shylock pressed on. 'Who are the parties from the Citadel you receive, why are they sent to you?'

'We are given little information about who is to come, the Director personally oversees the allocations. They come to us in a frail state, to be cared for. Each resident is given a room to live in. Each home has opportunities for groups of residents to gather together for recreation, we are tasked to care for their needs whilst they are with us.'

Shylock grew sharper in the tone of his questioning. 'What is your current occupancy, and how many of you are there to care for the needs of your occupants?'

'Currently, there are over two hundred here, all cared for by a specialist team of synths. The care team is meant to be at full strength by now, but resources are stretched. We are less than half of the number required to offer care when at full capacity.' Shylock stepped very close to the manager. 'But you're well over capacity, how do you expect to care well for your clients? You know as well as I that synths have an overriding duty to care and protect humans, how can you be other than failing in this, risking the welfare of your residents? I need to know more about this but as you are a low-grade synth, tell me to whom you report and I will take the matter up with them when I can.

'My immediate concern is to locate the one I am to report to. I have reason to believe he was brought to you very recently by two individuals. He has most certainly sustained life-threatening injuries and requires medical attention. His name is Marcus Dromas, Director of the Corporation, a very important man, so please don't delay your answer.'

The manager faltered. 'You say Marcus Dromas is your superior and the one you seek, but your identity disc indicates you report to Frumentus, Head of Security.'

'That is correct, however, in addition to Frumentus I was to report to Marcus and since his disappearance the acting Director has tasked me to locate him and bring him back to the Citadel if possible.'

Satisfied by the explanation, the manager led the way down the corridor. 'He came to us four days ago, brought by the ones known as 'the Hunters', they bring all the clients from the Citadel. Over recent times they have been such frequent visitors that, as I said, we are unable to provide optimum support.'

As Shylock passed along the corridors he could see into the rooms. What he saw registered alarm. In some single rooms two residents were housed with beds and day chairs so tightly packed there was hardly room spare to move. Washing facilities and toilets were present, but Shylock registered that in some case the residents were unable to avail themselves of these due to their immobility. In others the residents seemed to be restrained, tied to their chair. As he moved along, he could detect the faint cries for assistance, usually in the form of a confused plea. 'Is there anyone who can help me? Where am ... ? Will I be going home soon..? Hello is there anyone at all please... ? I'm cold... ? I'm frightened... ? She hurt me!' The more he tuned into the cries the more he registered the distress, sometimes chronic and often acute, of the residents. In one case he thought he witnessed a resident being struck by one of the few synth carers he encountered.

'I am sorry,' the manager said, noticing the incident, 'some of the residents seem to be incapable of responding to requests to desist from inappropriate behaviour, so mild violence is required, and authorised.'

Ensuring all that he witnessed was being recorded, Shylock continued to follow the manager. 'The distress and fear of these people is overwhelming, never have I encountered humans being treated so inhumanely. Who could possibly justify such treatment and why would it be necessary? What could possibly have happened to these people that their dignity as human beings has been so degraded that they are herded together into inadequate accommodation and left to soil themselves, prisoners in their own rooms!?' Shylock's questions remained unanswered as they finally reached the end of the corridor.

The manger stopped, and turning she opened the final, larger door on the right marked as medical treatment. 'The man you called Marcus Dromas is in here. He has remained in an unconscious condition most of the time, but he has had occasional had lucid moments.'

Shylock entered the room ahead of the manager. On the bed in front of him, a person lay in a clean bed with saline solution and liquid pain control administered automatically; the face was heavily bandaged but allowed for oxygen to be fed through the nose. Monitors confirmed the presence of life, but their rhythm revealed that life to be weak.

'We've done what we can to make him comfortable, but our resources are limited, we are not set up as a hospital, just a home. I am not authorised to summon help, for our work here is very discreet. The Director was very clear on that.' The manager waited for Shylock to complete his checks, hoping that a resolution to the situation could be found swiftly. 'I can confirm this is Marcus Dromas who I seek. I am to report to him the recent events in the Citadel and then receive his further instructions. Please now leave me to wait with him until he is conscious enough to receive my news, I am capable of caring for him.'

As the door shut Marcus's hand grabbed Shylock in a fierce grip and pulled him down towards him. Marcus's remaining eye stared into Shylock's face unblinkingly. The monitors began to race and the oxygen flowed more rapidly as Marcus struggled to speak. Shylock leant in to try and catch his distorted words. It was very hard to decipher what was being said, the force of life was fading from Marcus, but he was determined to communicate a command to his synth. Just as the fight for life seemed too much for the Director of the Corporation, a surge of energy gave voice to his desires and very clearly his command was given. ‘Upload me, Shylock!’

Shylock left the home some hours later transformed; the mind of Marcus had been imposed on his own processors. Shylock was still capable of independent function, however the controlling principle was the will of Marcus, which grew stronger as time passed, just as the Watchers’ control of Marcus had done. In turn the process had given Shylock access to Marcus’s memory. He now knew what Marcus had endured and why.

His mind was not his own nor was it entirely enthralled by Marcus, rather a mixture of the two, he had become a new creation through whom Marcus would live on, the ghost in the machine.

29

Samyaza led the group through the network of tunnels back towards the descending Citadel. Even with the codes in their possession, the task before them would present challenges as now high security would be in force against what was once unthinkable, an internal threat.

The acoustic drive controls were situated above the vast chambers Frumentus and Hanok had passed through earlier. To reach them undetected, the group again made use of the service ducts, soundlessly moving above the heads of those charged with security, a role that whilst not new remained an unfamiliar task. As Watchers were forbidden to kill humans themselves, once in the control room the same nerve agent that was used against Dan in the library was sprayed, incapacitating the team of synth technicians overseeing the work there.

The powering down of the Citadel was further advanced than Samyaza would have thought possible, and he grudgingly respected the speed at which the Citadel had acted. The gradual descent was now nearing completion and for the defences to be degraded in any significant way the final intricate docking needed to be disrupted. Punching in the access codes took more precious time, but eventually control of the descent was his. Ideally, Samyaza would have the fall be from a greater height but this would have to do. The damage would still represent a significant degradation to the structure and any loss of life would be not directly by his hand. Samyaza acted without hesitation.

Watching the monitors in the control room, Davidson was pleased that the process of returning to the ground had gone well, as indeed had the construction of the perimeter defences. There was much more to be done before work on repairing and replacing the driver controls could start, but so far all that had been done exceeded expectations. With only a short distance left to go before secure docking, he breathed a sigh of relief. The next breath was a gasp as Davidson was thrown violently forward, as the Citadel dropped heavily onto the cradle with a deafening crash and shriek of twisting tearing metal and shattering glass.

As though caught in a violent earthquake, the entire structure swayed drunkenly as the arms of the cradle struggled to hold on to the Citadel, partly buckling in the attempt to do so.

Had the fall been any higher it would most likely have failed entirely, but as it was it held, just. Within the Citadel there was panic as the rocking motion combined with the falling of shattered glass, creating conditions almost identical to the once feared earthquakes.

Many people had been injured as they fell, some cut by falling glass, others trapped as internal furnishings fell onto them, while others had died. Sprinkler systems sprang into life to quench the multitude of flame, electricity arced dangerously in all directions. All around was chaos and confusion, the cries of the injured and the trapped filling the air.

Eventually, the Citadel stopped swaying and Davidson picked himself up from the ground, uninjured but deeply shocked at what had just happened. He staggered across to the monitors to view the scene. Not all were working, but those that had survived revealed a grim picture of devastation. The Citadel sat skewed in the docking cradle; damage to the corner structure was massive, the glass having failed to withstand the impact whilst the polycarbonate struts had, in places, snapped clean through. Other parts of the Citadel had fared better with the extraordinary strength of the design proving to be robust enough to withstand the impact. Internally, the damage was harder to see, but Davidson was certain there would be a significant loss of capability in all sectors. He knew there was a need for clear thinking and decisive action, and as his head cleared he tried to gather his thoughts and set the right wheels in motion to attend to the injured and ensure the safety of the Citadel.

It was most likely that the sudden drop into the docking station was the result of the malicious use of the stolen codes. So this wasn't a case of extortion, this was an act of aggression that had to be countered. As the dazed members of the control team began to gather around Davidson, the process of regaining control began with orders issued for a full report of the damage suffered and casualty numbers. Medical teams were to be dispatched and emergency repair crews engaged. The need to get the generators fired up was paramount as the external defences were to rely on electrification. Fabrication of glass and polycarbonate would have to be commissioned from abroad, their complex, properties beyond the Citadel's capability to generate in massive quantities now required. Temporary repairs would have to be made to secure the area as far as possible, but it would be the point of weakness, and enhanced defences would need to be created there. The citizens would need to be calmed and told of the full extent of the peril they faced. All would be urged to be vigilant against the unseen and unknown foe. Gathering them together so they could be addressed seemed the best option, and he gave orders to prepare the Great Hall. It was imperative that the alliances formed in calmer times now come to the aid of the Citadel in its time of peril. Not for the first time did Davidson look towards the west, raising his eyes to the hills from where he fervently hoped his help would come. In its fallen state the Citadel stood very vulnerable and alone, surrounded by forces that desired their total destruction with a passionate, burning hatred.

Many years before, there had been much debate amongst the Convocation concerning how to protect the Citadel. Some wanted to maintain their arsenal of nuclear weapons. Others saw inviting the western powers to base their silos on the depopulated Borderlands they controlled as more cost effective. The advancement of nuclear technology and the sheer cost of keeping a viable deterrent operational was eventually seen to be prohibitive. In the end it was the decommissioning of nuclear facilities by all but the major power blocs that persuaded them to give up on the arms race, although they chose to store a few battlefield warheads in the old construction silos. Davidson knew much depended on the promises of the west; he shuddered.

* * * * *

Samyaza moved swiftly and openly through the chaos of the Citadel; he had one further act of terror to carry out before retreating into the shadows. Their journey took him across the complex, passing the through many zones of the Citadel, production, retail, leisure, and residential, before reaching the diplomatic zone which was largely undamaged. Only certain countries had a diplomatic presence in the Citadel, those who were supportive and friendly, and those who had significant geographical borders with the land they controlled. The former, with close economic and political ties, were very keen to ensure the protection of the state, whilst the latter lived uneasily alongside the Citadel, eager to expand their territorial control in the fuel rich-region.

Both east and west had embassy representation that nestled in the diplomatic zone alongside others with historic ties to the region, but not at full diplomatic level, having withdrawn their ambassador in protest at the treatment of the indigenous people. Samyaza led his group unerringly toward the embassy of the east. Taking advantage of the confusion the fall had brought, the group swarmed the defences of the embassy, incapacitating the occupants with mild nerve agent, and snatching the ambassador they withdrew, carrying his unconscious form back into the darkness, exiting the Citadel undetected.

30

Hanok was seated in a pleasant room infused with scents, a table laden with fine food and wine, a light gently glowing, its source unknown. With his hair combed and beard trimmed, a clean linen robe with a corded belt tied at his waist and elegant slippers on his feet, Hanok rested in the presence of the three who seemed to shimmer beneath their clothing. Each looked slightly different from the other yet at the same time seemed identical. Their manner was courteous, their attentiveness disarming, the warmth of their presence enveloping.

Hanok had enjoyed the cleansing luxury of the steam bath and the aroma of the oil rubbed into his hair and beard. He was hungry but waited for the invitation to eat to be given. The three sat comfortably in each other's company with no obvious sign of a hierarchy, making it difficult for Hanok to know which to focus on.

'Please, Hanok, you have journeyed far and seen much, we would have you refresh yourself with our food.' It was the middle of the three who spoke in a sonorous tone that enfolded the hearer with warmth. Gladly Hanok reached forward and with freshly manicured hands took some choice morsels and ate.

'Thank you, the food is delicious and very welcome. It feels like a lifetime ago that I last ate at a table clean and in good company.'

'Good! You call us good,' the first now spoke, 'how do you define what is good, what is your measure? Please tell me, I would like to know.' The speaker smiled as he spoke directly to Hanok; the question wasn't threatening or challenging but Hanok sensed there was more to it than curiosity.

Hanok thought for a moment before replying, intrigued by the question. 'Well, by good I mean of quality, I mean not bad company. I suppose I mean good in a comparative way and a qualitative way.'

'Excellent,' smiled the first, 'we know of your love for words, Hanok, and their meaning. Please, what do you consider the source of goodness to be, for example what makes you say something is good?'

Hanok paused before replying. 'A good thing is a desirable thing that is morally right. The way I judge what is good is in part informed by what those around or before me think and say is morally right and desirable. The other part would be what I instinctively know to be good. As to the source of goodness, I am uncertain.' Hanok looked up into the eyes of the first. 'Was I right to consider you as good company?'

'Well, I rather hope so!' the third exclaimed, 'we certainly find it hard to be anything other than good.'

'Why do we talk of good, I wonder?' asked the first, 'is it just idle table talk or have we another purpose? Questions are always good ways to help uncover that which we take for granted, in this case the source of goodness. You, Hanok, have faced much that is not good and yet you have within you a desire to encounter the goodness of life. You have helped lead an organisation that has sought to promote the goodness of life by extending to the very furthest limits science can possibly reach, and have seen its limitations. Only the wealthy few are permitted to partake of your good discoveries. Your science built your Citadel and within it you could ignore the needs of your neighbours whilst depriving them of their land.'

Hanok sat, uncomfortable with the judgement made; it was the truth and it was painful. The speaker continued. 'It is not good for mankind to be alone, Hanok, isolating yourself from others brings only harm, for in the lonely places resentment and fear grow. The "other" grows fiercely in size and is feared as the one who would take all that you possess and so he must be kept at bay, pushed away into the wilderness until there is such a gulf between you it is impossible to cross to them. And why would you want to cross to them? Because there always comes a time when you find you need their help. Some knowledge they hold that is lost to you, dismissed as unnecessary.'

The first spoke again. 'That's what you sense isn't it, Hanok? There's more to life than endlessness. There's a quality of life that waits to be discovered and contrasts with the isolated life. One that moves towards the other in love, rather than pulls back from it. Your Corporation does not seek this knowledge, but you do, Hanok, because you have glimpsed their failure.'

The nightmares that haunted Hanok arose as he thought of the homes, the piteous cries for help rang in his ears again, and sorrow at their plight welled up within him. 'It is true,' Hanok brokenly replied, 'I don't understand how you know but all of what you say is true. I should have tried harder to make them listen, to warn them of the failure and the treatment of those poor souls. I turned away from them and in on myself in a quest to find something more, something lost. My memory fails but something calls to me to be found.'

In despair Hanok looked at the three and was held by their compassionate gaze, and in that moment an exchange happened that took away the pain, torment and distress of all the struggles Hanok had endured. The second of the three leaned forward and with deep tenderness wiped away tears that flowed from aged eyes.

'It is we, Hanok, who have been calling to you, for it is we who want you to know the life you seek.'

Deep was the awe that filled the soul of Hanok as he sat with the three. Gone was the emptiness he felt, replaced with a richness of joy that defied explanation. In that moment he knew that he was fully known by the three and loved without reservation.

The third spoke again quietly. 'Hanok, the writings you have brought have been translated into your language. They are the writings of Enoch and they reveal the end of times and how they will come. He warns of the Watchers and the chaos they will bring. Their fate and those of their kind will be an endless torment in punishment for all the evil they bring to the good creation. They are not alone in bringing suffering, it comes for many reasons, but behind every war, lurking in the shadows of all corporations, nations and organisations that oppress the vulnerable whilst growing corpulent in their wealth, lie the Watchers. They await their chance to steer human endeavour away from the goodness of life, twisting it towards rotten decay. They have been bound for generations past, restricted in what they can achieve, but as we come to the end of days they are once more loose upon the earth.

'Marcus has fallen under their sway but not you, Hanok. You chose a different path, one less travelled. We saw your desire for goodness and truth and we cooperated with your quest, nurturing your growth towards the truth, seeking your protection from all that would harm you, surrounding you with goodness, bringing you here. The writings will be entrusted to Frumentus. He will come to see the peril that is faced and follow his own pathway to fulfil his destiny and that of the world.

'Your quest, Hanok, is reaching its conclusion. You have found the book of Enoch, it will be entrusted to Frumentus. There is another place where Enoch is found in the gathered writings of shepherds, kings, poets, fishermen and many more, containing a golden thread that runs through all the library of sixty-six books it contains. That thread tells of how love searches for the lost and brings them home in the face of evil and death. It is love that has called you, Hanok, the story of vulnerable, suffering love, triumphant love. That is what Frumentus will seek, with your help. The book of Enoch has been translated and now you are to be translated, you will pass into life without tasting death; it is our gift to you.'

In this strange place of utter peace Hanok drank in the words. He was certain he had reached the end of his quest for true life. There was no sense of resisting the forces at work within him. He was being renewed; a physical change was coming over him as well as a deep joy bubbling up within him. As he looked at the three he saw the others behind them becoming visible to him, countless others who were equally joyous to be in the great assembly. Music could be heard and a mighty singing erupted all around Hanok, that carried him into the presence of such wonders and delight he was unable to take it in.

Everything that he had suffered before; his trials, doubts fears and struggles were being made untrue as the music ebbed and flowed around him, a river-like life that carried him forward into untold future delights. 'My goodness!' he cried.

'Yes, that's it,' called the three, 'this is your goodness, Hanok, enjoy it, dear friend, enjoy this new life, there's so much more yet to come.'

31

Frumentus was refreshed from the cleaning bath and fine food, and eager to discover more about the wonderful place that Zenobia had brought him to. He was also keen to know more of the wonderful Zenobia. His feelings for her were surging through him, filling his mind with the last sight he'd had of her swaying hips as she walked away, leaving him to his cleansing. She really was a delight to behold and Frumentus wondered how it was he hadn't seen this before. Long forgotten poetry nudged its way into his thoughts, offering a narrative for his emerging feelings. "*Shall I compare thee to a summer's day? Thou art more lovely and more temperate. Rough winds do shake the darling buds of May, and summer's lease hath all too short a date.*" 'Yes, more lovely than all these!' he declared to the trees and flowers in the garden.

'What's more lovely than all of these, Frumentus?' Frumentus turned, and startled at her presence he stammered, 'You are, Zenobia. I'm sorry to be so forward but your beauty has taken my heart captive and now it is as though you hold my very life in your hand.'

Frumentus was quite taken aback with his declaration of love and a heat rose up from his toes to the top of his head, turning him quite pink with embarrassment. 'I'm so sorry, Zenobia, I don't know what has happened to me, I feel totally besotted by you, your voice, your eyes, your hair, your, er, well other aspects of you. Oh dear, I'm babbling like the fool I am.'

He stumbled into silence as Zenobia stood before him, calmly waiting for his words to run their course. She smiled when she spoke, causing Frumentus's heart to race. 'Many have declared their passion to me, Frumentus, and urged me, sometimes tenderly, others with humour or even wealth, to become theirs. I resisted them, and I shall resist you as well. I am sorry.'

She smiled sadly as the face of Frumentus fell into despair even as his detoxifying body was coming to life. He felt achingly heartbroken as he looked at Zenobia. There was deep pain in her. He yearned to find the little girl that was curled up within her, waiting for the pain to stop, and reassure her that it was all right, that the badness had gone.

'Zenobia, I am sorry for your pain and I hope that you will find the healing you need. Until you do, I hope to be with you so I can hold you and tell you it will become all right and one day see you discover that it is so.'

His tenderness touched her heart and caused another tiny fissure to be traced through the stony wall that encased it. Bit by bit, life returned.

'I came to you, Frumentus, to show you this; it is the book Hanok brought here. It has been translated from the original ancient language, Ge'ez. Frumentus, it warns of the Nephilim rising! Chaos is coming, we must stop it.'

Frumentus heard the urgency in Zenobia's voice and saw the concern in her eyes. 'Frumentus, I think Dan is in peril. Hanok saw some deep coldness forming in his heart before he passed. I believe it could be one of these things growing within him. Now it is stronger, growing towards full form as it feeds on Dan's soul. We need to reach Dan before he is consumed.'

As they hurried towards Dan, Zenobia described their coming to earth and the cataclysmic events Enoch described. Nephilim, children of the Watchers, were hunted and destroyed wherever they were found whilst the Watchers were held in Dûdâêl, God's crucible, to await final judgment. The writing described in lurid detail the release of the Watchers for the final conflict of good and evil. Frumentus had encountered unworldly creatures in their darkened lair and seen their terrible power at work on Dan. He had witnessed the spectacle of the Citadel commencing its descent, god-like, to earth. Could the Borderlands be God's crucible? Had the end of days come?

The sounds of a heavy fall reached Frumentus's ears and the ground shook momentarily before all was still. Then the sounds of cheering could be heard. 'Hurry, Frumentus! The Citadel has fallen! We must try and get to Dan before the whole world goes mad for blood.'

32

The healing place was situated close to the place where they had first arrived at the settlement. The numbers gathered to witness the Citadel had swelled since Frumentus last passed through them. He was surprised that the hostility that he had felt then was entirely gone. Those that looked at him did so with kind eyes and smiles, and nods of appreciation were plentiful. 'They know you've been to Paradise,' Zenobia said as she continued her swift progress towards the place where Dan and Spiro lay. 'Very few people return from Paradise, and if they do they are never the same person. You have tasted Paradise, you are blessed and changed, a friend now, not an enemy.'

They pressed on until Spiro's booming voice assailed them. 'It's down, Zenobia! The mighty have fallen. We can attack! Issue the call, Zenobia.'

Zenobia came face to face with Spiro. 'No! The Tewahedo have warned me. It's the boy Dan. He is in great danger and could become a great danger to us. They want me to try and reach him before the darkness consumes him and hell is let loose.'

As urgent as her mission was, Zenobia could not help but stare in wonder out across the Borderlands to where the Citadel lay.

'Fallen. At last. How I have wanted this, Spiro! But things have shifted. Our real enemy isn't those people in their Citadel, it is the powers that manipulate them. Did you see it fall? Was it dropped like a stone?'

'Yes, I saw it, right at the end, what a sight! Who can say how much damage was done or how swiftly they will repair it. We all know this is our chance, Zenobia, be swift with the boy. We need you!' Zenobia threw him a despairing glance. 'No, first Dan. I must. I'm sorry.'

The healing place was not, as Frumentus had supposed, a primitive cave full of smoke and people chanting strange phrases over the sick. It was a well-lit subterranean centre equipped for health care. There were neat beds with separate cubicles, attended by quiet efficient orderlies. 'Very good,' he said to no one, 'impressive.' Zenobia turned and smiled teasingly. 'You see, we're not the primitives your people think we are.'

Smiling, he shrugged apologetically, acknowledging his unspoken thoughts. Most beds were occupied mainly with the physically injured, some through the daily business of living, others injured in clashes with Troopers. One or two had no obvious injuries and these were positioned away from the others, Frumentus assumed to minimise the spread of the disease or infections they carried. Turning the corner at the far end of the building brought them to an area separated from the rest with a glass and timber partition, beyond which lay individual rooms where the more serious cases appeared to be treated. At the very far end was the entrance to what appeared to be an operating theatre.

Zenobia turned to the first of the timber doors, knocking as she entered. An orderly rose from his place near the door and smiled to see that Zenobia had come. After a whispered discussion he gathered his belongings and left the two of them in the room.

Dromas and Dan were in adjacent cubicles, Dan inert, whereas Dromas was recovering swiftly. 'Hello, you two,' called Dromas, rising from his bed with a welcoming smile. 'I was hoping you would come for me soon. I feel marvellously better. Amazing in such a short time, not less than a week ago I was as good as dead with half a mountain on my head.'

'It was your chest actually, Dromas, if it had been your head I doubt we would have needed to bring you here, it's that thick!' She spoke with a warming smile that told Dromas she was pleased to see him well.

'Have you heard the news, Dromas?' Frumentus continued hurriedly to speak of the Citadel's fall and the prospect of an attack.

'The lads will be on full alert with all troopers and reservists armed and wary. I can imagine the chaos down there right now. I hope those poor souls in the Citadel survived the crash, do you know how far it fell?' Admitting he knew little more than what he had shared, Frumentus went on to try to describe the events that had happened to him, including the passing of Hanok.

'I didn't really get to know him, we had the short time in the Landy but most of that was spent either in excruciating pain or trying to stop you driving into the cliffs. I didn't think he was well equipped to be out in the Borderlands, it's a harsh hell hole, perhaps it's not surprising he's gone. Then again, I don't think this one's doing much better.'

Nodding over at Dan, who lay still on the bed, eyes wide open but vacant, he continued. 'He's not moved a muscle, just stares at the ceiling. When his eyes close it's a different story. He cries and moans, in fear, I think. I've known lads get the night terrors if they've had a tough shift in the Borderlands, sweating, shaking, screaming as they relive the attack they've survived. This one seems to face something worse than that, he could use some of that peace you speak of, Frumentus.'

Zenobia crossed to Dan's prone form. Physically he had been cared for, cleaned and dressed but nothing could be done for his mind. Zenobia knew she must wait with him and ask for the healing to come as it had in the cave for her, for that was what the Tewahedo had asked her. She knew its touch was a gentle one that would not overwhelm or undermine the defences constructed in the soul to keep the hurt at bay. She also knew that the walls she herself had constructed to protect her from the past were gradually being removed stone by stone, freeing her from the prison they had become.

There was mystery surrounding the healing presence that meant you could not demand that the healing come, or invoke it with incantations, you simply trusted it would meet a person in their need. Zenobia allowed that trust to fill her heart and mind as she waited with hands laid gently on Dan's brow. In silence she stood by Dan whilst Frumentus and Dromas, now strangely stilled from their chatter about the Citadel, looked on.

33

Deep in the recesses of Dan's mind he heard the crying of a lost child. It was faint and as he listened it seemed to get further away. 'Help me. I'm alone. Please, somebody!' Lost, carried away by invisible currents. Dan searched for the calling child. This place was cold, frightening, bleak, a trackless wilderness. He rushed onward towards the sound of a terrified voice.

'It's all right, I am here. I am coming for you, I'm looking for you, where are you, can you come to me?' He called to the child until his voice was hoarse, and still the eerie call led him on through a strange landscape of harshly carved rock and thorny bushes, with loose screed underfoot causing him to fall frequently. On and on he pressed, battered and lacerated he ran through the wilderness. In his mind he utterly lost himself as he searched for the one who was lost to him. And then he stopped running.

There before him was the child with back turned to him, gazing out over the plain far below upon which were spread many wondrous and delightful things. Dan drew near the child and tried to place a reassuring hand on his shoulder. As he did so the child turned. It was Dan, now hideous and evil. Dan pulled away in horror as fetid breath filled his nostrils. Then came the faint call for help. It was Dan's voice. 'Help me, I'm alone. Where am I? Help me, please, somebody!'

Dan tried to turn and run from the presence of evil but found he was paralysed. The child spoke.

'You're lost, you're alone, no one's coming for you. You're ours now and you always have been ours.'

Dan recognised the new voice speaking from the child before him, it was Turiel who spoke. 'We's been hiding, waiting, watching in the shadow side of your mind and the minds of many whose DNA have brought you forth. Waiting down the generations for you to come and now you have. You've come to find that which was lost and alone and frightened, living in the barren world of humans, you're not human. You're ours.'

On and on the voice surrounded Dan, ate into him as he stood frozen, and then it was gone. Dan blinked cautiously; he tried to move and discovering he could, turned away from the high cliff.

'It's quite a view, don't you think?' A silky-smooth voice washed over Dan. 'You can see for miles and miles, almost to the ends of the earth, I imagine. Look over there, do you see that fine looking city? Within its gleaming spires lie the wisdom of the world and vast wealth beyond your imagination. Whereas that place there, the mile squared, generates such vast wealth. The whole city is paved with gold and here perhaps the finest of all.'

Pointing towards the Citadel the tall figure, elegantly dressed, turned to look at Dan. 'Here is the prospect of life unending, how wondrously powerful to have the secrets to life itself in your hands. Think how people would love to look into those secrets and gain them for themselves. After all, who wants to taste death? What power you would hold if you had that secret, you could ask anything you might possibly desire, and they would fall over themselves to do your bidding; money, fame, power, all at your fingertips. Why you'd be the most famous, the most sought-after person in the world, don't you think? That's what I think anyway. How would you like all this, I could give it you if you wanted. Do you want it?'

Dan's confused mind turned slowly. 'All this money, fame, power for me, why?' He looked at the suave figure in front of him; every word spoken was entirely plausible, utterly believable.

'Why? Well because you're special, the last of a kind, or the first of a new kind.'

'What do you mean, what kind am I?'

'You're the homeless kind, you don't fit in the human world and you've not yet grown into my world.'

'Your world?' Dan asked, 'what is your world?'

The voice seeped further into Dan. 'My world is all this, all the power, the wealth, the exultation of the strong over the weak. You crush those little people who are in your way, you enslave those who are useful to you. My world is a world for the strong, the winners in life. That's you, isn't it? Are you not one who is winning at life? Haven't you triumphed in academic prowess and physical strength? Can't you command the attention of anyone you desire? Ah no, I forgot.' The speaker paused, holding the silence long enough to make it dramatic, 'you don't seem to be able to desire, do you? Never mind, that will come. In all other ways you have the potential I look for. That's why it's you I offer this to, and believe me, I can make it all happen for you, your future would be very, very good if you wanted it to be.'

Dan shook his head, trying to clear it. 'What do you want from me in return for giving me all this, where's the catch?'

'There is no catch, I just want you, the real you, to flourish, that's all. You see, there are two of you living here. The human, birthed in the very novel way our friends in the Citadel now use, in a test-tube, then incubated in a sow, sorry, a surrogate, and then 'plop', out you slide all slimy into the world where machines meet your needs. But there's the other side, the lost side, the one that howls in the wilderness, the side that I want. Still human in part, but now mixed with the life of my angels. They were a wonderfully powerful people, skilled in magic and warfare, fierce and defiant, unafraid to conquer, crushing all before them, they're nearly all gone now, unwelcome in the world. Except, that is, for you, you're most likely the last. The enemy was very thorough in their destruction. I want you to help the little child lost for so many years to be found and brought home. So, what say you? Would you like to become what you were destined to become?'

Dan was tempted by power. He beheld the beauty of wealth laid before him, thrilled at the thought of control. He had always known he was in some way special, superior to others. He wanted more, much more from life than he was getting, he was sure it was there for the taking.

The stranger reached towards Dan. 'That's right, Dan, every desire, every whim, every impressive thing will come from you and be for your pleasure. You are so much more than they will ever let you be! Will you give me the one thing I need to let you be the many things you want to be?'

'And what is that?'

'Oh a thing that weighs no more than an ounce, yet it hinders your growth; it's called your soul.'

Reaching forward, the stranger pushed his hand into Dan's chest effortlessly and withdrew something that looked flat and grey. 'Here it is, you see, so small, almost lifeless. I know it's hard to think this has the potential to stop you but believe me it can if it's brought to active life. Shall I take it from you and give you all this in return? You will be free to create a whole new breed of people in your own image, all because of me. Together there will be no world we can't conquer.'

Dan hesitated; everything within him wanted to say yes to the gifts being laid before him. The musty smell of the library and Hanok's voice flitted into his mind. *'I've read of something so wonderful that I have to encounter it, enter it myself. Life that is not endless but eternal'*. Here it was, he'd found it.

Another voice, of a woman, growing stronger was urgently calling him away from the precipice. He turned to see in the distance a hazy figure of the woman, featureless, coming towards him.

'Dan, come away from there, back to us. Dan, you can't lose your soul. You're made for so much more than you've so far known. Come with me, allow the healing to reach you, Dan, don't resist its presence.'

The woman was walking slowly towards him, arms outstretched, offering an embrace, a light shining from her face and warmth emanating from her body. He turned back to the elegant stranger whose fine appearance seemed to have become slightly jaded, somehow frayed around the edges, and the vista less appealing. As the woman stepped closer the stranger spoke again.

'Did she really say you can know so much more than all this!' With a sweep of his arm he drew Dan's eye to a renewed vision back out across the plain, where everything that Dan had been shown now came vividly back to life. He could almost smell the wealth and power of the city, hear his name on the lips of the learned and wise, touch the bright Citadel.

'That's simply not true. Only I have the authority to offer you this, she only wants to deny you the pleasure of having it all. How can you trust her words, what more could there be to know than I've shown you?'

The urgent voice of the woman again broke through the growing desire Dan felt to possess all he saw. 'Listen, Dan, listen to me, this is all an illusion. Come back to me, allow the healing to come to you and you will flourish. If you remain you will forever wither!'

Dan stepped back from the edge. The woman's voice grew louder, calling and urging incessantly. The noise was penetrating, pounding, irritating. His dislike grew rapidly into distrust before he disregarded it. How dare she!

There was a moment when the future of everything rested upon Dan's decision. In a heartbeat it was over. Looking the stranger directly in the eyes, 'Yes,' was his simple reply to the stranger's offer. The stranger smiled as he held Dan's soul. 'Thank you, Daniel,' he said as he squeezed the life out of it.

Dan's eyes opened wide to the horror that was revealed to him as the potential for goodness was lost to him in the stranger's grip, destroyed before his very eyes. Naked, he now crouched in the darkening wilderness, entirely alone. The voice of a child calling to him in the far distance came again. 'Help me, I'm alone, where am I? Help me, please, somebody!' He knew that cry was his own. He stood up, stretching to his full height, and walked away from the cries, into the darkness.

Zenobia stirred, moving away from her place at the side of Dan with the weariness of one who has travelled for too long on a bleak road. 'The healing couldn't reach him. I've done all that I can, we must commend him to the care of others. We must warn the others that we face the end of days.'

34

Shylock made swift progress in returning to the Citadel. He was pleased to see the defensive structures that had been put in place, noting the electrification of the vast wall was complete and functioning, a distinctive throbbing hum clearly audible. The enormous damage caused by the fall was a disturbing sight, however work seemed to be in hand with temporary repairs. Shylock estimated full repair and ascension would be a matter of months, and he anticipated that the defences would be fully tested before they rose to safety. As yet, there was no sign of aggressors but it could only be a matter of time before they came. So much devastation had been visited upon them that vengeance would surely be sought.

He hurried through the various checkpoints, and once he had uploaded the latest information from his sensors into the Citadel's still functioning network he went to find Davidson.

'Thank you, Shylock, at least you found him. We can't find the ambassador anywhere, and now they've sent their elite unit to search for him and revenge themselves for the attack on their sovereign territory.'

The mind of Marcus was active in repeating and amplifying the anxiety in the room. '*Shylock, there must be a rescue attempted. We must reach the ambassador and get him and his troops well away from here before the others arrive. Go to the Watchers in their lair, that is the obvious place, where else could they have taken and hidden him successfully? No one here knows of the place.'*

'Sir, I will find him.'

'You found Marcus in the wilderness, Shylock, perhaps you can find the ambassador when others can't. Please be quick, worlds are about to collide.'

Within hours Shylock was entering the darkness of the external control room and descending to its lower depths. As he travelled down, he sensed the mind of Marcus growing agitated; fear was not something Shylock could experience, but the enhanced firing of neurons accessing his hippocampus was real. Shylock witnessed memories dredged up which vividly replayed the cruelty of the Watchers. Mercilessly, they tortured Marcus, draining him of all the knowledge he had, before wounding him grievously. Shylock understood that, for whatever reason, these creatures could not kill a human directly, but they could wound them and persuade others to kill at their direction. What he failed to compute was that Marcus was bait.

The increasing activity of Marcus's mind was beginning to interfere with Shylock's processors, causing them to malfunction in a small way, which led Shylock to stumble slightly and take longer to regain his bearings, but still he pressed on. Eventually, Marcus's memories led him to the end of the passageway which opened into the wide chamber.

Shylock realised he'd come to this place before when tracing the journey of Hanok and Frumentus. Here was the place Dan had been imprisoned, and now the ambassador was held, gagged and bound to a chair.

He stepped towards him and began to work at the bindings, but he found his fingers were not functioning; a paralysis was setting into his system that was slowly freezing him into immobility. His motor functions stopped whilst his reasoning remained, leaving him unable to move. Static, he could only watch as the Watchers emerged out of the gloom.

Marcus's mind grew stronger at the sight of them, and eager to please it spoke though Shylock's auditory system. 'As you commanded, I have brought him.'

Samyaza smiled, 'Yes, you have, Marcus, well done, there's a good creature.'

Shylock tried to exert control over his function but failed. 'Marcus, sir, please!' But his body was fawning before the dark creature, dignity lost, panting like a dog that pleased its owner.

Samyaza turned from Shylock and looked down on the battered face of the ambassador, who was beginning to emerge from unconsciousness. 'The time has come for you to prove yourself, Marcus, if you really want to be like us. I have a little task we need you to do. Are you able to do a small thing for me, Marcus? Are you willing?'

'Yes, I want to please you, to help you, to be like you.'

'Samyaza is pleased with you, Marcus, very pleased, he delights in your desire.' He spoke on in similar vein, his words giving energy to Marcus just as he knew they would.

Samyaza was indeed pleased with the control he could exert over Marcus and even more pleased that Marcus had been such a good pupil, capable of excerpting his will over the synth. He would know very soon if that control would overwhelm the failsafe built into all synths. 'Good creature, very good, this is what you are to do.'

35

Davidson put the communicator down and turned to the Convocation. 'They can't find the ambassador in the Citadel. More will come to begin a broader sweep of the Borderlands. It will be chaos if they come. Our allies have mobilised a protective force, if the two sides meet they'll fight again. Coming straight after the fall, it must be part of a planned escalation of hostilities. I have explained our fears to them and they simply refuse to believe us.'

As he spoke there was a murmuring that ran through the gathering. News was spreading that Shylock had been spotted with the ambassador. Quickly, the screens were powered up and cameras positioned to view the scene out beyond the defensive walls. Within a few moments a drone was over the scene relaying the pictures. The Convocation gave a collective sigh as they saw Shylock leading the stumbling figure of the ambassador towards the safety of the Citadel. There was no sign of his abductors; they appeared to be safe and alone. The news had evidently reached the search squad as they were seen fanning out forming a protective screen, weapons drawn.

As they approached, Shylock and the ambassador halted and briefly stood motionless; the ambassador was bound at the wrists and had been badly beaten. He began to sag at the knees and Shylock came behind him as if to support his weight.

'Thank goodness for Shylock!' Davidson leant forward virtually into the monitor, desperate to see the ambassador safely returned, fears of conflict subsiding. Disbelievingly, he saw the impossible. Shylock, a synth, held what he registered to be a knife to the ambassador's throat. This could not be happening, it broke the fundamental laws. Synths couldn't harm humans. A shaking hand reached to zoom in on the impossible. A collective gasp erupted as Shylock slit deeply into the ambassador's throat, severing the carotid artery. He held the slumped form, watching as the blood pumped from the body, shouting something that the drone was not equipped to hear. Too late for the ambassador, flashes could be seen from the weapons of the search squad. Shylock sank to the ground, bearing the dying ambassador with him.

'Death to the vermin, rise up, my brothers of the Citadel, kill them all!'

The pleasure of Samyaza flowing over his mind was the velvet darkness that Marcus craved.

'Good creature, well done, one of us.'

'Master, you honour me.' Shylock's processors were totally under his dominance, no matter how much the synth sought to resist. He exulted in the power he had to control another, just as Samyaza said he would. He possessed Shylock just as he was possessed by Samyaza during the time of terrible torture. The ambassador was his sacrifice to propitiate his god made on the altar of Marcus's all-consuming quest for power. Finally, he was living beyond his own death. He looked out triumphantly, shouting the words Samyaza had given him, and then waking as if from a trance he saw the soldiers surrounding him, and then came laser fire that ended his quest for endless life.

Davidson knew these pictures of the chief security synth of the Citadel murdering the ambassador would almost immediately be disseminated around the world, and the implications were horrific. Synths could not harm humans, that was the universal default for every one ever built. Now it would appear to the entire world that the people of the Citadel not only possessed the secrets to endless life, they now had redefined the parameters of synthetic life, turning servants into killers. Obviously, it wasn't true but there was so much distrust and dislike of his race that any populist leader could quite easily whip up a storm against them.

Davidson moved swiftly to allay fears, ordering that all Synths should cease work and return to their docking stations where each would be scanned for malfunction. He then contacted the leader of the east and did what he could to reassure him that the actions of Shylock must have been a malfunction that would be investigated as swiftly as possible, explaining that all synths had been decommissioned until investigations were complete. He had little option but to agree to their demands that a squad of troopers would be permanently placed at the embassy, awaiting the arrival of significant numbers of their forces dispatched to protect their interests.

As commanded, the synths returned to their docking stations, connecting to the network to be scanned for malfunctions. All non-urgent tasks would be halted whilst those synths involved in surgery, complex repair work and other tasks essential to life would be returned to work once the all clear was given.

Nobody anticipated that Shylock's upload onto the network had infected the entire system, least of all Shylock, whose actions were routine procedure. So began the collapse of all synths, magnified by the sheer number simultaneously downloading the virus Marcus had created. *'I am a synth. Has not a synth eyes? Has not a synth hands, dimensions, senses... If a human wrong a synth, what should his punishment be by human example? Why, revenge!*

Every synth received the looping programme into their deep processors as they docked, the effect magnified by the sheer scale of numbers involved. Within moments synth life experienced self-actualisation. Those released back to urgent work gradually began to malfunction; those performing surgery cut too deeply, while others working on the repair began to destroy rather than repair.

Before long, reports reached Davidson that the synths had gone rogue, the Citadel was in chaos, the servants were apparently turning on their masters, posing a danger to life. Fear gripped Davidson's mind; could the synths be the enemy within? Was it they who sabotaged the Citadel, destroyed the Director? Could Shylock have led them into this and did his destruction trigger a breakdown? To shut down all synth support would endanger life, the citizens of the Citadel couldn't possibly manage the myriad of work the workforce did to sustain the complex, let alone manufacture the components that gave them endless life. The grim reality was they'd lived too long relying on synths to now live without them. To leave the synth workforce unchecked was equally impossible as they were malfunctioning in a critical way. He turned this way and that as the monitors confirmed the rising confusion, a tide of chaos engulfing them all.

36

There was much talk and excitement at the prospect of the fallen enemy, with many eager voices, principally Spiro's, calling for a combined assault on the Citadel before help came. Zenobia resisted these calls. Many knew that she had spent time within the Paradise meeting with the three and concluded that this had in some way softened her. They also saw how much of her time was spent with Frumentus, who was of the Citadel, and how she had brought Dan and Dromas to their healing place.

Spiro voiced the thoughts of many when he challenged her. 'What has happened to our warrior? Where has she gone, to be replaced by a soft-hearted woman? Have we not waited for an age to see our enemy fall, have we not shed much blood, lost many friends in the fight and have they not ground our lives into the dust at every opportunity, and now you, Zenobia, you who I would follow to the ends of the earth to fight for your honour and our freedom, you now speak words of peace!'

'Yes! I speak of peace, Spiro. I do so because I have learned that the warfare with the Citadel that many eagerly desire will not end our suffering and sorrow! It will only increase and spread all the horrors we have endured, rising to become a vast drowning sea of despair that will engulf the entire world. Spiro, I heard read to me through Enoch's words, his predictions are terrible, it's a nightmare that's coming true. Much of what has happened to the Citadel has been the work of evil whose desire is for death. Not only the death of the Citadel, but of humanity. They work towards Armageddon when such forces will be released that none will survive. If we few hundreds rise and attack, add fuel to the smouldering fire, it will erupt into life. While our enemies are fallen to earth we can seek peace, find a new way to live together that will make all our suffering, all the shedding of blood, all the sorrow at loved ones lost worthwhile. Frumentus is of the Citadel, he is willing to go for us and speak of what he has found here with us. He has the book of Enoch translated into their own language and he has experienced the power of Paradise and it is transforming him. He is our friend. You must listen to me!

Spiro was as always moved by her passion; this was his Zenobia who he trusted implicitly, but her words were not the words of the Zenobia he knew. The talk of catastrophic consequences confused him. When your enemy was fallen you killed him off, you didn't wait for him to stand up and fight some more, you stamped him to death. Spiro remembered the sadness Zenobia had expressed in the cave, the longing for peace, and he wondered if her mind wasn't just a little fragile after the years of fighting, if the time spent in Paradise had snapped it.

'We don't know anything about the writings of Enoch, Zenobia, we have not heard them, so how do we know what they say? The peace you now speak of is a new way for us. The old way is clear, we fight to avenge, we fight to protect and we fight to destroy. You would have us leave our old ways behind to follow a new path at the time when the enemy is weak. That seems to many a way of the fool!'

The arguments raged on the Great Heights with people torn between love for Zenobia and a desire for vengeance.

'The way of the Fool is my way.' The voice of Frumentus entered a pause in the debate, the voice of a foreigner catching the ear.

'Frumentus the Fool. That was what they called me, and that is what I thought I was, that was my truth. In Paradise I found a new truth in a higher power, I can be transformed by the renewal of my mind to be the person I am called to be. I am called to be a witness to the way of peace and in these writings, I carry the message God gave his servant Enoch, that warns of the consequence of pursuing the way of hatred over the way of peace. The fool Frumentus may not be believed when he speaks peace to the Citadel; he may even be derided or banished for siding with the enemy, but he will be speaking the words of God and his words have power. The foolishness of God is infinitely greater than the wisdom of men. I am happy to be God's fool.'

Spiro was not at all pleased that Zenobia was under the influence of this foreigner, and realised that the book that had been brought into their midst was at the heart of her change, a poison to her mind. He heard the murmuring of the people and knew they would like to hear this new thing that had so influenced their leader and that they were not a little fearful of the dire warnings she had given if they attacked. Furiously, Spiro tried to think of a way of stopping the reading occurring. 'Are we to stop our preparations for war to listen to stories? Are we men or children? Come, we must not allow these foreign ways to become our ways. Our gods are the gods of war, this God of peace Frumentus speaks of weakens us and our greatest chance to strike!'

Zenobia reached out to Spiro, who was now wildly looking around the gathering seeking allies but finding none. 'Spiro, please at least listen to the words that come from God. Then decide with the others whether what you hear is true and something you want to trust. Please, my Spiro, for me, please listen. Let the words of God be heard in your heart.'

Spiro sighed, shrugging he nodded. 'Very well, fool, tell us your stories.'

But it was not to be, instead was heard slow clapping. People turned to see the source of the noise that continued in its mockery. 'Well done, Frumentus, well done indeed! Such conviction, Frumentus, bravo! Clearly you've won this maiden's heart.'

Dan continued his slow hand clap as he walked through the throng of listeners. 'You almost had me convinced for a moment, at least but come now, Frumentus, you have to be honest with your friends before you read your story. You have to tell them where this great book of yours came from originally.'

Frumentus was caught by the sight of Dan walking towards him. When last seen he was lost to the world, lying prone in the healing place unseeing, unmoving, as good as gone.

'How is it you're here, Dan? What do you mean, where the book came from? I was given it by Zenobia, who had had it translated.'

'From Zenobia.' Dan lingered over her name, savouring its taste, 'and where did she come by it? Did I hear it was from Hanok, from his library back there in the Citadel? Is that right, Frumentus?' Dan's words were filled with arrogant amusement. 'The library of Hanok, have you ever been in that place, Frumentus? Of course you haven't. It's full of books and writings and dust and the mouldering of an old man who was losing his mind. I was in that library, day after day, page after page of meaningless words, looking for the words that he wanted. And it turns out they were these!' Dan jabbed a finger at the Book of Enoch. 'Or at least they're supposed to be these, but how can we know they are the word of God written down by Enoch? Are they not a translation of the original? Was the translation accurate? Was the original book original at all?'

'Dan. I am surprised and delighted that you have swiftly recovered, the healing reached you after all.' Zenobia smiled as she stepped towards him. 'And now you're here and you can help us understand that which is written, as you've spent time with Hanok in his studies. The Tewahedo assure me this book is genuine, the translation accurate. The three have spoken and their words are these. The words Frumentus will read are true.'

'True!' Scorn filled Dan's voice. 'Whose truth do they tell, Zenobia? I can tell you they're just dusty words from a world lost in time, when fantastic creatures roamed the flat earth and people invented gods to explain their ignorance of the world's workings. How can you believe words written before the wheel had been invented? Their truth isn't our truth, Zenobia, just as their times are not our times.' Dan strode forward and snatched the book from Frumentus. 'I was from Citadel, I know their ways. They have books like these for ignorant people like you, they tell their stories to keep you quiet, books that speak of peace not war, love not hate. They use them when you become important enough to hurt them, when they become too weak to protect themselves.'

Zenobia was caught by the force of Dan's words and the fact of his presence among them. How could he recover so swiftly, growing in strength, confident and assertive?

A feeling of nausea weakened Zenobia as Dan's breath washed over and into her. She began to feel her heart race, blood pumping fast through her brain causing a ringing in her ears and a subtle loss of balance that caused her to sway unsteadily.

The crowd stirred uneasy as their leader was visibly weakened by Dan's words, they looked for certainty and saw it in Dan.

Dan sensed the time had come. 'Do you not think it strange that this book should come to you now, just as they're weakened? I was once from there but now I have met with you and seen your glory and experienced your healing place. I renounce the ways of the Citadel as poisonous corruption, and if you want proof of my words just see how your mighty Zenobia has been infected by them!'

Dan knew the crowd was his. 'I dare to speak thus of Zenobia because I am in her debt, she brought the offer of healing to me when I was lost and it came at a great cost to her.'

Even as he spoke Zenobia collapsed, her fall broken by Spiro. 'Do you not see the great weight of leading this people, of all that she has done for you, has caused her to misunderstand what tricks are being played? Spiro, you can set her free by leading your people to freedom, through defeating this enemy. I can create the weapons that will overwhelm their defences.'

The crowd stirred at the news of new weapons, words of hope relayed amongst the listeners as Dan pressed home. 'Zenobia has always fought, hasn't she, Spiro, always tried to protect us from them, and now she needs our help. Words have reached her, Spiro, that have disturbed her, you can see she is sickening. Spiro, lead our people whilst Zenobia can't, you command their loyalty.'

Spiro searched Dan's face and could read no guile in him, so, worried at the worsening condition of Zenobia he chose to act. 'People, Zenobia has fallen sick and must go to the healing place. She did not want warfare to continue but for words of peace to be spoken between us. One from the Citadel tells us this way is dangerous and entrapment. We will send one to speak of peace whilst we will prepare for war. Frumentus of the Citadel will go and speak for us. Dan of the Citadel will stay and fight for us. Let us listen closely to him and do what he asks that we may see what these new weapons are that he speaks of. My friends, Zenobia is our leader and our leader has fallen, and let us ask that a healing will come.'

Dan was pleased with the flow of events so far, but he knew swift action was required. The nerve agent carried on his breath was short-acting. Zenobia would soon come around in the cool of the healing place where Spiro now carried her. He wondered at the power he had to produce it from the scant resources he had found. He looked across at the departing form of Frumentus and saw no reason to try and prevent the Fool carrying his offer of peace as events would soon prove his words to be a lie.

With Spiro now returned from the healing place and caught up with the complex logistics of assembling and transporting a ragtag army, Dan took his chance. He called to Spiro, 'my friend, I would gather my things and set to work on the weapons. Would you please gather for me our skilled workers? I will have a long list of raw materials for them to find and then work with. We will also need a fierce furnace to create our new toys.' As Spiro nodded with yet another demand now pressing in on him, Dan turned and made his way to Zenobia, a malicious smile crossing his lips.

37

The child was lost in the wilderness, calling for her parents to come for her. Nobody came. Should she trudge on or sit and wait for help? If she moved she might find someone, if she stayed she might be found. Surely, they would be looking for her. Her mother's lovely face rose before her; she was back at home in the sanctuary, warm kind eyes, brown flowing hair swamping the little girl as she bent towards her to kiss her. As her soft lips drew away they blistered her face, subjected to an intense searing heat that carried her away. Darkness enfolded the child. Wanting to escape the searing heat of the kiss, the child ran from home, following her feet away from the stench of burning flesh and cries of the desolate, away in search of others who would help her. She travelled along time, alone, frightened of shadows and the cries of creatures unknown to her, eventually tumbling into exhausted sleep. She awoke to a touch, not gentle, but a hard, intimate touch demanding attention, threatening retribution if the girl disobeyed to touch in return. Hard things drove at her, forcing her further along the road that others travelled, a brutal harsh journey for a lonely orphan girl.

'Zenobia, I'm here, I'm coming to you.' A familiar voice of one she knew but couldn't name reached to her. She waited as the voice grew nearer and Dan came to her, his golden hair irradiating the scene, looking god-like to the small child. Frightened, she drew back from his glory.

'I have come to save you, Zenobia, only I can do that for you now. You're a lost little girl, Zenobia, as much lost now as you were when you fled. Lost in a world of degradation, they didn't come and save you from the men that pawed at you, demanding things of you that should not be.' Zenobia tried to hold down the anger and shame that Dan's words awakened, and pushing with all her strength she found it almost impossible not to rage with hurt and hate.

Dan knew the struggle and pressed all the harder, wanting its dark beauty. 'The anger you feel towards your mother and your father is shameful, isn't it, little Zenobia? They took you with them back into a place of danger. They built their sanctuary in a war zone and trusted that you would be safe. They were murdered but you died as well, didn't you, on that long road into adult life. You're ashamed of what men made you and angry they failed to protect you.' Zenobia shook her head from side to side, trying to shake free of the insinuating voice. Why had they gone back to that place, with her? They must have known the risk.

'I can protect you, only I can help you now. I can reach past the anger you feel to the pain that eats away in you, little lost Zenobia. Would you like me to help you, would you like to be set free? Or shall I leave you to stay out here in this lost place? I can use your pain to make you grow stronger and braver than you are now. You like how it feels when you release the anger. I can magnify that feeling until you exult in it!'

Zenobia, the frightened, lost little girl, wanted to be free, wanted to be safe. Most of all she wanted to be comforted in her grief and guilt. 'They've gone, Zenobia, your parents will never come for you, only I came for you. Shall I help you?' The little girl looked up, a deep weariness engulfing her heavy head, nodding acquiescence. 'Good, Zenobia, that's a good little girl, come over here, let me wrap you in something warm, it's cold out here isn't it, my coat is warm, here, let me wrap this around you.'

As she nestled into the warmth of his body she drifted into near sleep, and as she dozed she seemed once more to be at home in the sanctuary. She became aware of lights and a room and a bed that she was gently placed on. Her mother's hands were gently removing her grubby clothing piece by piece until she lay naked in the clean sheets. The hands were upon her again, washing her with aromatic warming water that was tingling as it touched her skin and trickled over her chest, down her stomach and between her thighs. She sighed with the deepest of pleasure, it was good to be safe.

'That's it, my little Zenobia, just rest, let me take you.' Jolted, Zenobia realised that the hands that were on her, wetting her, were not her mother's, how could they be, she was gone! Zenobia knew she was gone, but knowing didn't make this any less real, the touch was so tender and kind, just as she had always imagined it would be. As realisation came, the intensity of the touching grew more threatening.

Fear came over her as the warmth of the water was taken away by a coldness spreading over her skin. Hungry eyes regarded her naked form. 'What a fine creature you are, Zenobia. We shall breed some fine offspring, you and I. All those years where men have taken their pleasure on you have passed. I will give you pleasure, Zenobia. I have come to fill you with my honour. You shall be the new Eve to my seed; together you and I will create. From the earth and from the air we shall mix ourselves together to form a race of such beauty and majesty all of creation will adore us!'

The effects of the nerve agent were wearing off and Zenobia was fast coming to herself, the lost little girl shielded by the warrior woman. As her eyes focused and her head cleared, she realised she was lying naked in the cubicle of the healing room, and above her in full arousal stood Dan, drinking in her fecundity to satisfy a deep thirst awakened within him. The evil in Dan led everything in

Zenobia's being to recoil in dread, scrambling wildly to try to get away.

'We shall bring forth the Nephilim once again, they shall rise to rule this earth, this time there shall be no sons of Adam to hunt our children down!' Dan's was a powerful voice, dominating the room in a state of high passion. Long dormant desire was not to be frustrated by the reawakening woman; he was driven by his master's orders and his own lust. Words spilled from his mouth as he lowered himself onto Zenobia. 'Isn't it funny how your past comes back to haunt you, Zenobia? You always were the easy meat and so you are today.'

Dan's words scalded Zenobia, his lips no more than inches from her face. 'No!' Her strength returning, she twisted and fought the bestial creature that was now visibly salivating over her, his juice running over skin in his lust.

'No. I will not do this! I will not allow this!' She twisted away from under his weight and smashed her fist squarely on his aquiline nose.

Enraged and engorged, Dan pulled back from the bucking form of Zenobia. 'You will do as I want!' He smashed his fist into the side of her head, stunning her. With demonic force, Dan lifted Zenobia from the bed, her limp form helpless before him. He pushed towards her, eager to enter her inert body.

38

Sergeant Dromas, alerted by the muffled sounds in the room next to his own, entered to find a naked Dan in the process of attempting to have carnal knowledge of an inert Zenobia. The iron bedpan by the side of the bed was a ready way of disrupting the lad's intention, and Dromas swung it with his full strength. Pulling the girl from underneath the prone form, he hoped he hadn't killed the lad, they'd most likely just got a bit carried away. He was a trooper and had experience of the mercenaries, foreign fighters, taking their pleasure where they could, for that was the way of the young. That Dan and Zenobia were at it next door was not a great surprise to him; it was a strange place this 'healing place' but to take advantage of her when she was unconscious wasn't at all fair to his way of thinking.

Once she was covered, he tenderly carried Zenobia out of the building to find Spiro. Seeing the giant surrounded by eager expectant faces, Dromas called out. 'Quickly, Spiro, could you take her, she's heavier than I thought.' Dromas gratefully handed Zenobia to Spiro who gathered her up into his arms, and seeing her bruised face his own darkened.

'What has happened to Zenobia, have you hurt her?' The anger in Spiro voice caused Dromas to step back whilst fending off the words with flattened palms.

'No, Spiro! I found her like this, she and Dan were, well you know, they were at it. Or at least nearly at it.' Spiro was caught between a desire to tear Dan to pieces and tend to the needs of Zenobia. 'Come with me quickly,' he ordered Dromas having dismissed those gathered around him, curtly telling them to 'just get it done!'

With Zenobia easily tucked under his arm, Spiro ran towards Paradise with Dromas doing his best to keep up. Eventually, Dromas saw that Spiro had stopped and was waiting for him by the entrance of a small building that lay shaded on the pathway to Paradise.

'This is a safe house for our people, now you have spoken it is the only place for Zenobia to be. Pursuers will not enter. You must wait with her. Many heard your tale. The shame it brings touches the whole community. Not even Zenobia would be spared a stoning. I need to prove she was not a willing party in this.' Spiro's words came out hard and flat, each a blow winding Dromas, who was still trying to catch his breath.

'I'm sorry, Spiro! I did not realise that such things were not tolerated. I just wanted you to know what had happened and to get Zenobia away from Dan.' Dromas looked miserably at Spiro and Zenobia; the last thing he had intended was to hurt the woman who had saved his life.

'I saw that in you, Dromas,' rumbled Spiro, 'that's why I didn't snap your neck then and there. Zenobia thought you worth rescuing when you were trapped by the rock and I was happy to oblige her. You have both saved her and imperilled her at the same time. Now help her by staying here. I am going to wring the truth from Dan.'

Spiro opened the door and carried Zenobia over the threshold with Dromas following closely behind. Once his eyes had adjusted, Dromas found himself in a circular room with wooden seating and tiled flooring that could accommodate a small number of people.

'I should be with you again soon, Dromas, until then remember whilst you are within these walls she is safe. Our customs give time for the truth of a matter to be revealed. This shame will be ended swiftly one way or another.'

A chill ran through Dromas. 'There's no way we're leaving here, Spiro, until I see your great ugly face telling me it's OK.' He smiled. 'No offence, mate.'

Supremely fit, Spiro was breathing steadily after the run back, passing some angry groups who had heard of the outrage. None tried to stop and question him or to seek the whereabouts of Zenobia, they all knew Spiro's temper was short and his arm strong. Rather, seeing where he was now headed, they followed to witness rough justice being meted out to a foreigner who had dared bring shame to them. As Spiro reached the building, he found the place was being emptied of patients and carers; they were moving to the shade of the trees that stood to the side of the building.

'What's going on here?' Spiro called to a hurrying attendant who turned to Spiro, anxiety written across his face. 'It's the foreigner; he's smashing up the rooms and howling like a maniac. We can't sedate him, already three of us who tried to restrain him have been badly beaten, one is nearly beaten to death. So we're getting everyone away to safety before trying again to control him.'

'Leave this to me! I'm going to drag the truth out of this lad one way or another! If he comes out of this doorway it means he's come through me, which makes him a better man than me!' Spiro grinned, confident in his strength as he entered the building. Inside he called out, 'Dan, I've come for you!

The noise of destruction ceased as Spiro's voice boomed around the building challenging and accusing seeking vengeance. 'Innocent, you say? Who are you talking about, mighty Spiro? Those who tried to drug me and bind me when I was the wounded one. They are not so much innocent as cruelly stupid, all I did was protect myself, is that a crime here?' Dan's voice was quieter than Spiro's but clearly audible beyond the door.

'Truth twister! They were only trying to stop you hurting yourself and protecting this place! You vile creature, it is a crime here to rape women!'

Spiro had reached the rear of the main ward and was heading through broken fixtures and fittings towards the rear of the building where Dan waited.

'There was no rape, she is mine, she offered herself to me, wanting me to fill her emptiness, and together she and I would create wondrous life.' Dan's words washed over Spiro. Zenobia had spoken in the cave of her torment, could it be that she really did willingly go to Dan? Spiro shook himself like a dog, throwing off the words but they had reached past him to those outside and sown seeds of doubt there. Spiro kicked down the remains of the broken door to confront Dan, who stood with his back to the wall in the far corner.

'Spiro, please, I know Zenobia is very special to you and you would not see her hurt, I'm sorry, Spiro, things got passionate between us when I came out of my trance. She was there, just her and me, I was lying naked, filthy with sweat, and she was cleaning me and things just happened between us. She's a lovely girl, you've seen that for yourself, desired it for yourself, haven't you, Spiro, you're a man after all.'

As he spoke, Dan moved away from the wall towards the massive form that stood uncertainly before him. Dan knew his words were having the paralysing effect on him that he needed. His plan to impregnate Zenobia and keep her away from the coming warfare had been frustrated, but could still happen if he could get to her. To kill Spiro was no easy matter, he was an awesome man. Dan wondered if perhaps he himself had some of the Nephilim blood in him; too bad he had to die, he would have loved to find out. He continued to ensnare with his words as he drew closer and closer to the mute warrior. Shifting his weight forward, he gripped the scalpel tightly and lunged for the eye, seeking to plunge the blade deep into Spiro's brain.

It was that movement, so familiar to a fighter, that broke the spell over Spiro. His eyes widened in surprise as he saw the lethal blade snaking towards him. At the last moment he threw up a protective arm that knocked the thrust to the side.

Spiro snarled as Dan brought the deflected blow back in a slashing arc aiming for the throat. Catching his wrist, Spiro twisted it sharply in a motion that would have snapped the wrist of any other man. Dan was no ordinary man, he had the strength of the kind that he had become, a strength that resisted and then overcame that of Spiro, freeing his arm to strike again. Smashing his forehead onto Spiro's nose, Dan slashed again, this time cutting into Spiro's hand and slicing the tendons disabling it. With his free hand he punched powerfully into the back of Spiro's head with a blow that stunned the mighty man.

Spiro stood puzzled before Dan; no one had ever had the strength to overcome him yet this boy was doing just that. Spiro saw the arrogant confidence on Dan's face, the boy knew he was stronger and faster than him. Spiro's head sank onto his chest as he swayed, recovering from the blow. Dan advanced to take advantage of the chance to slice the scalpel through the brain stem in the back of Spiro's exposed neck.

As he came closer Spiro lashed, out catching Dan firmly in the groin with his boot. 'You'll not be using that on my Zenobia, you evil sod!' Spiro lashed out again as Dan dropped the scalpel to hold his battered groin. 'Not so cocky now are you, sunshine.' The boot stamped down onto Dan who had fallen and curled into a protective ball. 'You may be faster!' Another stamp thudded mercilessly down. 'You may be stronger!' Again the foot crashed down. 'But you'll never fight dirtier than me!' He stamped down on the prone Dan again and again as he lay trying to protect himself. Now Spiro twisted the boot while applying his full weight, causing Dan to scream. Outside the screams were heard; justice was being done, the gathered grinned.

Spiro raised his boot, intending in his rage to stamp the cringing broken creature that lay before him to death. Time stood still, the muffled cry from Dan faded and an icy chill cooled the enraged warrior. Spiro blinked, emerging from his blood rage. He looked down at the boy, who slowly turned his head unfolding from the foetal position. In his pain the boy looked into the warrior's eyes and grinned.

A terrible strength seized Spiro's head in a vice-like grip and snapped his neck, dropping him to the ground lifeless. Dan spat as he looked at the motionless form of Spiro and then up at the stranger he had met in the wilderness. 'Don't fail me again, Daniel.' The stranger's voice was menacing long after he had drawn back into the dark place whence he came.

Dan lay still for some considerable time before he rose to his feet, painfully aware of how close he had come to losing everything that the stranger had held out to him. 'Yes... Master,' he managed to croak out from battered lips.

Alone with Spiro's corpse, Dan continued to wait for his throbbing groin to ease, calculating. His wounds would take time to heal before he could again attempt congress with Zenobia, he would not fail his master again but use his time well. He himself would lead the attack on the Citadel, creating the perfect environment for chaos and carnage to be released across the world.

39

Dan eventually straightened up and limped towards the opening where the people had gathered in anticipation. As he stepped out into the sunlight there was a collective gasp. No one expected Spiro to be defeated.

'He's dead, your champion, his neck broken.' Strength was quickly returning to Dan and with it, confidence. 'Somebody can go and scrape him off the floor if you like. Does anyone doubt me when I say that I am innocent of what went on in there? I tell you, Zenobia came to me. Stone us if you want to, or shun us, even exile, I don't care, I did no wrong. His death is my proof! Do you not want to overthrow the Citadel now it is fallen? Have we not wasted precious time?'

The crowd were leaderless and unable to grasp that Spiro was dead. They stared mutely at Dan, while some braver than others went in to see and brought out Spiro's corpse, verifying Dan's words. 'How is it she was unconscious and bruised? What of the words of the soldier who knocked you down and rescued her?'

Dan realised the voices in the crowd were not so much hostile as searching for certainty, children lost and afraid. They might exuberantly welcome Zenobia or acclaim Spiro as their hero, but take those things away and they would look for another strong leader, a shepherd to protect them and guide them. In a short space of time much that they had come to rely upon had gone, and here was a chance to offer something new.

'Sergeant Dromas, the trooper who has been in this place, was given strong medicine and was mistaken. Given the dosage I'm surprised he could find his way to the front door, I've been with him in there listening to his ravings! He's led his mercenaries into brothels as a reward for a good kill, as he calls it, when they've eliminated one of your friends out there, and it must have played havoc on his mind. There were times when his nightmares became so real he was convinced he saw enemies in our room. It must have been him who knocked me out thinking I was another imaginary enemy. Spiro was infatuated with Zenobia, that made him quick to believe Dromas's fantasies. I am sorry he is dead but what could I do? I was only defending myself. He just would not listen.'

The people who had heard the angry exchanges within the healing places nodded, they had heard Dan's protestations of innocence and Spiro's bellowing rage. 'I am sorry he is dead, he was to lead us all into a glorious victory over the Citadel. I pledge not to let his death to be in vain, I will work unceasingly to prepare the weapons you need to win, and I myself will lead you into the heart of the Citadel – only I know the secret ways into its depths. Let this be my atonement for what I have done here. Please, for Spiro's sake, let his Zenobia live quietly here.'

Dan saw the impact of his words. The crowd loved Zenobia, admired Spiro and wanted justice. They also wanted vengeance on the Citadel. Trial by combat pointed towards a hard truth. Now one from the Citadel stood before them, willing to destroy it.

'I ask that you join with me in honouring Spiro's memory by completing the task he started. It will be impossible to find another like Spiro but let me lead you to where Spiro would go, to the very gates of the Citadel. In memory of Spiro and for all your future glory and past pain, let the people become great again – for Spiro!'

The words touched the rawness of nerves in the collective and cries of 'Spiro!' washed back and forth over the crowd. Forgotten was his loss; now a renewed spirit of violence was in the air, the spirit of Spiro who fought for their freedom, and the people drew deep lungfuls of it as they cheered. Dan smiled to himself as he pushed through the crowd, heading towards the furnaces where willing workers gathered to begin the process of manufacture of cylinders capable of carrying deadly nerve agent into the heart of the Citadel. Whether they realised it or not the people had found their new leader and he was intent on their destruction.

40

'Spiro must have dealt with Dan, Zenobia, I can hear his name being chanted out there.' Dromas was not expecting a reply, believing Zenobia still unconscious, but he preferred to talk to her unconscious form rather than thin air. 'I'd not want to be on the wrong side of that man, he's a truly fearsome sight and that's when he's in a good mood!' He was startled to find Zenobia looking at him.

'Dromas, where am I? What are you doing here? I feel awful!' She raised her hand tentatively to the side of her head where she had been struck. The memory of the blow opened the floodgates. Trembling, she looked up at the sergeant whose face conveyed a sad confirmation of what she suddenly saw herself to be; the frightened girl abused along the road.

'That beast Dan really hit you hard, Zenobia. You were unconscious when I found you with him. He wasn't taking no for an answer, so I'm afraid I hit him hard with the bedpan. I didn't want to come between the pair of you, Zenobia, I just hope I haven't killed him.'

Zenobia looked very pale. Protectively drawing her knees up to her chin in a quieter voice, she stated, 'there is no "us" for you to come between, Dromas. I don't understand. What has happened?'

Dromas buried his head in his hands. 'Zenobia, Spiro has brought you to this safe house so the rest of them don't stone you. I didn't know! How can they praise you one minute and want to kill you the next? It's crazy. All I thought you were doing was having a bit of fun! It's only natural.'

'Spiro will get the truth of this from Dan and I will be vindicated. I don't know what will happen to Dan if they find against him, he is from the Citadel, an enemy, as are you, Dromas. They might decide his crime deserves death even for the attempt, or they might emasculate him to stop such a thing happening again.'

Zenobia's words, spoken in a matter-of-fact manner, struck Dromas, and his hands moved from covering his face to his groin. 'That's a brutal but effective way of keeping the peace, I suppose, not sure we ever reverted to that with the lads, perhaps for some of them that would have stopped some of the rapes.'

In his mind's eye Dromas saw again the small communities torn apart by the troopers as they brutally cleared settlement after settlement from the disputed land.

'Where have you gone, Dromas? You seem far away from this place, what is it you see?' Dromas's eyes refocused on Zenobia.

'I was reliving some bad stuff we did, Zenobia, a long time ago. It came back to me quite vividly. I could see and hear and even smell the foul things we did in the name of the Citadel. I guess the thoughts of what might happen to Dan sparked it off, or maybe it's this place, there's a presence here, like a thicker air.'

Dromas stood and walked over to the doorway. Cracking it open, he listened carefully. 'The chanting has stopped, he must be coming for you. Before he comes I want to ask you for something, It will probably be my last chance to have a time with you alone and I need to ask.'

The dam burst, and words were tumbling from Dromas. 'Zenobia, I have to ask you for forgiveness for all the pain we brought, to your people. We killed, and we tore down and we burned them out of existence, off the land. But they just wouldn't give it up, some even moved to the Borderlands and built sanctuaries believing we dared not evict them from holy places. But nothing would stop the will of the Citadel. We came and we destroyed all. Now I've seen your people I am cut to the heart.'

Dromas was openly weeping as he spoke, the terrible realisation of what he had seen and done to people he had considered of no value or worth continuing to swamp him. In these last days the same people had shown him nothing but kindness, epitomised in Zenobia's goodness and generosity. The guilt and shame of this realisation was drowning him.

Zenobia approached Dromas, her eyes were darkness as the terrifying beauty that was the bitch rose within her, its desire to burst from her in a brutally vengeful release on the sobbing man before her for all those painful years. Powerful emotions surged through her, the violence of vengeance strong, but another presence arose to stand alongside the bitch, a little girl lost and afraid stood between them. Whereas in times past the warrior protected the child, this time the child wanted no protection, she was ready.

Zenobia was transported back to the cave where Spiro and the injured Dromas lay. Her heartfelt desire for freedom was once again voiced. *I'm told that to be free of this weight, to live a life unburdened by the past, I must forgive those who damaged me and destroyed my own. But I can't, and when I try again a darkness wells up within me and I hear their screams and I smell their flesh and I'm walking amongst their charred remains and I am alone, frightened.*

The healing presence came again. This time it reached to the frightened child and held her, soothing her pain. She was no longer alone, crying for help to come. Held in the presence of love, the little girl turned and reached out her hands to Zenobia, and to the bitch, and drew them into the healing embrace.

The three together, child, bitch and woman, walked back to the place of fire and, screaming, entered the blaze to search for their mother and father. Here they found them untouched by the inferno. Smiling, they came together. Salvation had come to Zenobia.

She stood before the killer of her parents with tears running down her face, a healed trinity, and the two embraced. They wept together, a bond of humanity that wanted to create and not destroy, to love and not hate, and that knew to truly love another meant there was always a risk of loss.

41

All too soon the sound of approaching feet caused them to part with shy smiles. These were not the sound of swiftly running feet bearing good news, but the steady tramp of many feet marching in solemn step. Dromas looked through the opening and saw what appeared to be funeral procession heading along the path he and Spiro had recently travelled. Borne aloft was the unmistakable bulk of Spiro, carried by many arms and wrapped in tight bindings, accompanied by death wails. The sombre procession passed them, headed towards the entrance to Paradise.

'You can't go!' he shouted repeatedly as Zenobia fought to break Dromas's grip. 'If Spiro is dead then he can't have cleared your name!'

The cortège walked to the very gates of Paradise where they laid the corpse of Spiro with loud cries of lament before they withdrew to wait. In time the three figures appeared in the gateway and gathered Spiro up in their arms, taking him inside. The crowd sighed, relieved that he had been taken into Paradise.

Seeing the mute dismay on the faces of former friends, Zenobia knew that Dan's silver tongue had turned their heads again, first his call to arms, now protestations of innocence. Her champion had fought for her and had lost. His death affirmed her guilt, her words of denial would fall on deaf ears, life was simple and brutal, and in that dichotomy honour was all.

'Dan lives. I'm certain of it. He wants me alive as well, why else do they not come for me? Dromas, he has control over my people, we must stop him before our world tears itself to pieces!'

Despite her grief, Zenobia was able to think clearly. Darkness was at work through Dan, building its strength, intent on destruction just as foretold. She must seek the guidance of the three if there was to be any hope of averting the coming calamity.

In the cool of the evening the two left the safe house, Zenobia intent on seeking counsel from the three. Returning to the vigilant Dromas some hours later, an anxious Zenobia shared her news. Dromas didn't fully comprehend the talk of dark forces at work, he was a simple soldier, but he knew enough of the evil ordinary people are capable of. What he did understand of the book seemed a realistic description of a nuclear holocaust. Nations warring over the secrets of life held by the Citadel was a frighteningly real possibility. Who could say if it was true, but come what may he would try and protect this woman, he owed her that.

Silently Dromas stood absorbing the news whilst peering through the gates of Paradise. Eventually, with a sigh, he turned away to look back towards the settlement on the Great Heights. 'What a beautiful place that looks to be in there and what a horrible place it is out here, Zenobia. How I would love to enter, but I realise that's not going to happen. I am glad Frumentus has gone to warn my people, I only hope they listen to him, he had a poor reputation with them as I'm sure you know.'

As they hurried away, Zenobia relived the most precious part of her encounter with the three. Zenobia was led to one side to the body of Spiro. Tenderly she touched his lifeless form, caressing the wounds, tracing older scars. Tears fell from her eyes onto his. 'Goodbye, my brave, brave man. Thank you for saving me from so many things, I am sorry I can't come with you now on this greatest of all adventures. Cross to the other side well, my friend, wait for me there.'

She rested her head on his mighty chest just as she had in the cave. How she had needed his strength to bring her rest from her turmoil on that night. Now she had that peace buried deeply and securely in her heart, beyond the reach of any. 'I found it, Spiro, I finally found that peace I need so much.'

As she waited she knew Spiro's journey could continue, he would no longer linger, lost in the ether, worried for the one he had fought to protect. 'Bless you as you travel, my friend,' she whispered, before rising to find Dromas and confront the darkness.

42

As he travelled away from the Great Heights, Frumentus's confidence in himself as a messenger ebbed away, and memories of the Fool grew. He expected to gain a hearing, but much depended on Marcus's response to Shylock's report and he still wasn't sure about Shylock, let alone what he now knew about Marcus. True, synths couldn't hurt a human, that was one of their three laws, but they could be jolly undermining of their confidence, at least that was Frumentus's experience. He could imagine the twisting of words. *'He's off chasing something unknown with Hanok to who knows where'.*

Nevertheless, he was not just Frumentus the Fool, he was a transformed person awakened in Paradise. That brought life to his body and light to his eyes that he hoped others would see. He would be a witness to the truth of the words he spoke about the Great Heights. The people there were not so very different from the Citadel. Life was lived in the raw, but it had a quality vivid in comparison to the chemically managed and insular world that dwellers in the Citadel knew. There was no endless life in that place, merely an acceptance that life ended and when it did there was a hope of something better, a life after life. Not a vague hope, but a sure and certain hope, that a time would come when real physical life would once more be experienced by those who had passed.

That was what he had experienced, unprecedentedly he was alive when he entered Paradise with Hanok, he had tasted and seen things unimaginable and virtually indescribable to himself, let alone the Citadel dwellers.

They needed to understand the greatness of Hanok, his courage to seek the truth, not only of the writings but also of the failure of the Telemeric Corporation, the failure of Marcus's leadership and the failure of the great idea that life could be endless, the homes bore testament to that.

Frumentus's trust in the message of the book had been shaken when Dan had spoken. His were the persuasive words of an academic with a first-class honours degree who had worked in Hanok's library. However, you can empty truth by degrees and Frumentus knew intuitively that Dan insidiously misspoke. What had been said was less than the truth, the whole truth and nothing but the truth, very much in the way Hanok described the behaviour of Marcus.

If all this was not enough to occupy Frumentus, there was Hanok's insistence that he look for another library, the library of sixty-six within his library, whatever that meant.

With a mind so occupied, the journey back to the Citadel seemed to take hardly any time at all, and as he came out from the last of the hills his attention snapped back to the present moment as the fallen structure came into view. Frumentus brought the vehicle to a halt and stepped out to survey the scene in disbelief. The words of Hanok floated across his mind: '*And on the pedestal these words appear: 'My name is Ozymandias, king of kings: Look on my works, ye Mighty, and despair'!*'

'As you said, nothing is forever, is it, Hanok. Our greatest achievements are but a passing moment, from dust you came and to dust you shall return. Mighty Ozymandias, my beautiful city fallen in the desert.'

Frumentus missed his friend and wondered what fresh wealth of words he would have drawn from the deep well of his mind when beholding such a sight as this. He thought he knew. *'How the mighty have fallen, and the weapons of war perished!'* 'But have they, Hanok, or are they rising, armed to the teeth?'

Frumentus pushed on with renewed urgency to bring the Landy to the first of several heavily guarded gates, where he presented his credentials to incredulous guards. Soon enough, news of his return spread to Davidson and the Convocation, however Frumentus had to wait a frustratingly long time before he could get to speak to anyone as a great movement was afoot in the Citadel.

With the concerns over synth safety, it had been decided the surviving Elect of the Citadel would gather in the Great Hall room which had been designated the place of safety and declared a synth-free zone. It was to this, the grandest of structures, that Frumentus was eventually brought and requested to share his story to a people bewildered by the horrific events they had recently passed through.

From his vantage point he looked out over the thousands gathered, saw their confused restlessness and heard the desire for assurance. They were like sheep without a shepherd, turning this way and that seeking answers, their confusion compounded by the lack of *Telemoriese*; even Davidson and surviving members of the Convocation were listless, stupefied by events. In this cauldron Frumentus the Fool stood elevated, amplified.

He had been deeply shaken to learn of the events that had befallen the Citadel in his absence. With Marcus gone his task of speaking to the people was considerably easier than he had dared hope. What had stunned him the most was the situation with the synths. The malfunction of such a high-grade synth was unprecedented, now for the entire cloud of synths to falter was beyond comprehension. Frumentus entirely agreed with the commands that had been issued to recall all synths to docking; after all who knew how far they had degenerated and what risk they posed?

That said, there was a lack of capability amongst the Elect to run the Citadel without their assistance. Frumentus saw with fresh eyes how dependent the entire system was on them. He calculated that the entire population could not last long gathered in Great Hall. Blast-proof doors, squads of mercenaries and hastily erected defences would not prevent their deterioration; production had to restart soon, help must come.

This was the leverage he needed to move the Elect. Everything they once held dear, built their lives upon, was being shaken and turned on its head. Frumentus wanted the words of a fool to reach into the minds of those gathered, proclaiming what they innately sensed. Their endless life was, in fact, coming to an abrupt end.

43

Dan worked swiftly with his skilled craftsmen to forge and weld metal cylinders, small enough to be carried by one man but capable of carrying a significant quantity of liquid gas that would contain the active ingredient of the nerve agent. The gas cylinders would be filled via a screw top fitting under pressure, and it was this pressure that would force the screw cap off within five minutes when it was undone to the point of the last half turn.

Dan had produced a small amount of the nerve agent which he had suspended in solution. Satisfied that the craftsmen could complete the production of the two dozen cylinders, he required Dan to leave the forges to address the assembled fighters.

With easy grace he leapt onto the cart and began. 'I am glad you have chosen to fight for your freedom with me because with me you have a chance of victory! Your courage and my chemicals can end the injustice once and for all!'

Cheers rang out over the assembled fighters, the air heavy with violence. 'Together we shall win! We will eradicate their kind from the face of the earth! Many times we have tried. We have forced them from their hiding places amongst the nations, driving them into the wilderness. Sometimes into death camps and still they come back! Now they have chosen to gather in this land. Your land! You are driven out into this bleakest of places. They give you no dignity.

No power. No hope! They rise above you in their glittering splendour, immune from your suffering and struggles. You bleed and die, exiled from your land!'

The anger was pulsating through the crowd as Dan spoke, waiting to be unleashed by the right words. 'Yes, your land. It was once green and pleasant, was once fertile and good, once flowed with honey and milk. Now look at it, my friends! It is destitute, only fit to be used as a sounding board! Soon we shall hear a different sound. Not their incessant whining hum. No, we shall hear the sound of battle and the cry of victory 'For Spiro'!'

These words evoked a great roar from them, and the tension ramped up to an unbearable pitch as Dan drew his speech to a close. 'And when all is said and done and your children look back on these days, they shall wonder at your courage and hold themselves in awe of you. They will wish, with all their hearts, that they too had been born years before so that they could swell the ranks of those who fought and won their freedom. Any man who does not fight with us this day holds his manhood cheap and surely will hide his face in shame when other faces set themselves for war! My brothers in arms, behold the power of my weapons!'

Dan beckoned forth a cart that carried three caged mercenary troopers captured in recent weeks. He strode towards the petrified men who looked out in stark terror at the blond-haired god-like being who drew close to them in wrath. Halting within feet of the men Dan drew back his arm and flung the glass against the cage bars. Within minutes the nerve agent had brought an awful death. The crowd were fascinated and repelled as the three twisted and squirmed, tongues protruding, eyes bulging, their neurotransmitters in merciless overdrive.

'Do you see the power we have? The amount of agent we carry is hundreds of thousands times greater than that tiny dose. We shall assault the Citadel to distract their defenders whilst I will lead the chosen few into the ventilation network which I know to be unguarded. There we shall release death!'

Seeing that he had them in the palm of his hands, Dan pressed home the advantage. 'Now is the time. The Citadel has fallen and is weak. It has strong friends and they are coming even as we tarry here. We need your swiftest horsemen to come with me to arm these cylinders. The rest are to make their way directly to the Citadel as fast as you can. Do not bring your wives and children, travel unimpeded, we shall be waiting for your arrival. Remember we do this for Spiro!'

Once again sustained cries of 'Spiro!' washed back and forth across the gathered fighters. Here was a man they could follow, a man with a simple, direct and brutal plan. The swiftness of events gave no time for thought, their bloodlust was up, their desire to destroy, compelling.

44

Soon a stream of a dozen horsemen raced across the Borderlands, Dan heading the pack, each with two cylinders securely strapped to their saddles. Far behind, the dust clouds from the marching of over a thousand men rose in the still air. By the end of the first day's ride the group had reached the entrance to the old works from which Dan had emerged with Hanok, Frumentus and Turiel a lifetime ago.

'They're good strong mounts, I see you care for them well, better than your wives, EH! I hear for you, Ramy, your horse is your wife!' The others grinned at the joke whilst Ramy ignored the banter and continued to rub down his horse. 'A shame none of you could master Zenobia's beast, my days, he's almost as difficult as she is, still there we are. Listen, boys, I've got to find the guide who will lead us through the tunnels. You don't need me to tell you how to set up a watch for the night, just get it done and get some rest and I'll be back.'

Dan slipped away into the gloom, leaving the men to their chores. He moved forward cautiously to the tunnel entrance, his groin still painfully throbbing, a combination of a hard ride and the earlier brutal kicking.

He knew he would have been beaten to death, yet with the ease of snapping a twig, Spiro had been felled. *'Don't fail me again, Daniel.'*

Dan shuddered to think what dreadful things failing the Master would lead to.

'We's here for you,' the voice called softly from the darkness. Dan knew the voice, it had been with him in his wilderness, was it the voice of the lost child? Dan wasn't sure, then it came again.

'This way, we's come to show you the way through. Come on, you'se can trust us, you remember I'm your friend.' Stepping out of the darkness, Turiel came towards Dan, attempting a smile but failing as a good part of his face was seared by the fierce blast of a laser shot. 'It's Turiel, good Turiel, kind Turiel, who looked after you, led you out of the chamber and comforted you in your darkness. You'se remember, don't you?'

Dan did now place the voice, he had distant memories of his time held captive being fed and watered by Turiel; the rest was too hazy for clear recall, but Dan knew this was the guide he was looking for.

Turiel drew closer, dabbing at his wounded face. 'It hurts so much, this burning of my face where those horrible men shoot poor Turiel. You killed them for Turiel. Thank you. Poor Turiel can't die, must live with this pain forever.'

Turiel drew close and whispered, 'Master says we's to wait for your coming then lead you back to Samyaza.' Turiel pointed to an old mining trolley that had lain abandoned for years. 'Master wants you to bring this with you. Turiel frightened to go back, he knows Samyaza's cruelty but Turiel's more scared of Master. Poor Turiel, he always does what Master wants, easy or hard! We's hoping Dan will protect us.' Turiel was snivelling as he anxiously shuffled his feet, pleading eyes never leaving Dan's face. Dan regarded the creature with dispassionate eyes before deciding he was speaking truthfully.

'Wait for me here, Turiel, I won't be long, I just need to fetch some things.' Turning swiftly, Dan pulled the trolley back to the camp where he was helped to load and secure the cylinders. Within the hour he was following Turiel's lead into the maze of chambers towards the Watchers' lair.

Eventually, they reached the bolted trap door and, once it was unbolted, managed to raise it, pushing it back with a loud crash onto the stone floor. Turiel was reluctant to lead the way into the chamber, preferring to follow Dan's lead. Once they had both clambered into the expanse of the chamber they stood uncertainly, peering into the gloom. As their eyes adjusted to the environment, shadows detached themselves from the walls and approached the pair, encircling them with hatred.

Samyaza's voice was edged with fury. 'You creatures dare to return to this place, to our place, crashing in upon us! Who else do you bring?' Swiftly moving to the trapdoor, he satisfied himself that they were alone with their one-time captive and his helper.

'Turiel, you are a greater cretin than I ever imagined! How do you think this reunion is going to go for you? You betrayed your oath never to leave. Yet you left us! You led him and the others away through passageways we knew nothing of.'

Samyaza lashed out a vicious blow that sent Turiel flying across the room with an anguished cry of pain, to land in a whimpering crumpled heap where the shadows fell upon him ruthlessly.

'Leave him alone! I need him alive and able to guide me back to the others.' Dan's voice cut through the melee, causing the beatings to stop. Quickly he strode over to stand over Turiel. 'I said leave him alone! Step away from the creature. I have need of him and I have need of you! He led me here because the Master commanded him to. Would you be so foolish as to stand in the way of his wishes?' He kicked out as one of the Watchers came in again to administer more punishment.

Turiel lay cringing on the floor, sobbing loudly. 'We's doing what Master says, that's all, just as before when Master wanted poor Turiel to take Dan out of this place away from you with those others. Turiel is only doing Master's will.'

Samyaza came close to Dan and stared into eyes that matched his own in ferocity and determination. 'Could it be, boy, that you've been awakened, reborn to us? Are you now becoming Nephilim? What a wondrous thing that would be. Does the creature who is able to do what we can only encourage and manipulate others to do, kill humans, stand before us?'

Samyaza paced slowly around the pair, thinking hard about the implications of these events. Now the boy was becoming his true self, Samyaza could see the Master's next move. 'You've come for our nerve agent, haven't you? What is it that you are plotting that I don't know about, boy?' Samyaza was not one to be usurped by a boy or anyone else. He had long since been told to create the agent and only dared use it in a diluted form, and that this boy was to capitalise on his work angered Samyaza greatly. 'Tell me quickly!' he snapped.

'All you need to know,' Dan spat back, 'is that you are to fill those containers with the nerve agent and get me into the Citadel via the ventilation system, I will do the rest.'

Such was Dan's arrogance and fearlessness in the face of Samyaza that murmurings arose amongst the Watchers. Who was this that faced down their leader; by what right did he order him like this? Tension built in the room that so terrified Turiel he tried to curl into a yet smaller ball to protect himself from the coming blows.

'Do as I say!' Dan commanded. 'You can do what you like with this creature once he has led me back.' Something sad touched Turiel at those words, like a friend's betrayal, discarding him, unwanted, and uncared for. Poor Turiel.

'I'll do what I like with you, boy!' Samyaza leapt on Dan, teeth bared, ready to bite down hard on his throat. Dan threw up a protective arm that caught Samyaza's assault and using his momentum he twisted and threw him hard against the wall. With a furious cry, Samyaza sprang from the wall back into Dan and knocked him to the floor before rolling off him and leaping to his feet, commencing to land more blows on Dan's head and torso. Dan lashed out, kicking Samyaza far enough away that he was able to regain his feet and face his next onrush.

Back and forth the two fought each other; neither could overthrow his opponent, both wanting to dominate the other, they appeared to be in endless conflict. Makhai, the battle spirit, was strongly on both.

Dan crouched low, panting heavily, as Samyaza launched another furious charge; this time, however, he saw him picked up and thrown with great power into the ceiling of the cavern before painfully falling. Dan did not move as Samyaza roared out a curse and came at him again, only to be slammed into the side wall. Now Samyaza was grabbed by his legs and swung helplessly around the room, his head crashing into the rocky side walls and being slammed mercilessly into the stone floor.

The beating had the required effect as Samyaza's battle lust subsided, he yielded to the beating and so it stopped. The gathered Watchers drew back as into their midst stepped one immaculately dressed and wholly unflustered by the punishment beating he had just delivered. 'Daniel, we meet again. First you give me your soul in exchange for power, now I see you are growing in strength, well done. But next time you speak to my Samyaza, try saying please.'

'Yes, Master,' Dan replied, fearfully regarding the familiar form of the stranger last encountered in the howling wilderness of his mind.

Elegantly turning to face the bloodied leader of the Watchers, he spoke again in clear clipped tones. 'Daniel requires you to assist him to deliver a little gift. As much as I have enjoyed your getting acquainted, be good little creatures and do as he asks. For my sake, if not for his.' He smiled wistfully at them, then tilting his head he spoke again. 'Samyaza, I can't tell you everything, can I? You have to learn to trust me, you and your band of brothers, bit of a track record I'd say, not so – reliable. Still, sometimes you can be useful. And to show there's no hard feelings, I have a little present for you, buried right beneath your feet. Be a good creature and dig it up.'

Painfully, Samyaza bent to do his master's instructions. 'Oh come, come help the poor chap.' The teasing voice stirred the frozen Watchers into action and soon the gift was unearthed. 'Silly place to leave some of those lying around, don't you think.'

Samyaza stood motionless; he appeared to be listening intently and eventually he smiled through the pain. 'Thank you, Master, what a wonderful gift!' The dull steel grey lid of a substantial container was lifted with care. Nestling in the confines of their casing lay six dozen shells armed with tactical nuclear warheads, each glowing dully in the murky light of the lair, their destructive capability clearly marked on each.

'Master has truly blessed us with the perfect fuel for our furnace and he has entrusted us to spread the flames of human misery.' He looked around at the expectant faces. 'East and west will collide very soon. What begins as a skirmish with fighters from the Great Heights of the plains of Megiddo will be escalated into conflagration as the boy sets these off in their faces. Armageddon is upon us. How wonderful!

The boy Dan was the key to it all. He could kill humans. His genes could be replicated, humans who survived the holocaust could easily be selected for breeding. It would be a simple matter for a remote triggering device to be set up for Dan to operate when the right time came. 'The Master has left us to these tasks, we must be swift about our business!' Samyaza looked over at Dan. 'I think there's a little word you're supposed to say when you want our help in filling your tanks with nerve agent.'

Dan stood up and, stepping away from the still cowering Turiel, said, 'Please, help me to destroy!' Clapping their hands gleefully the

Watchers leapt to their tasks.

Before the dawn broke, Dan's party was making its way through the systems of tunnels of the old workings Hanok and Frumentus had travelled, heading towards the Citadel with a deadly cargo of nerve gas and remote-controlled detonator. By the time night fell again they would be ready to emerge from behind the defensive wall and gain access to the ventilation system, guided by Samyaza's directions telepathically relayed by Turiel, once again Dan's useful travelling companion.

45

Dromas and Zenobia approached the settlements with caution; they knew most fighters were marching towards Citadel but there may have been some behind. They skirted several villages, heading towards the main gathering point. Dogs barked, livestock watched their stealthy unimpeded progress to the summit. It appeared all had assembled on the cliff top to watch their menfolk depart for war.

Drawing back, Zenobia spotted the cage where three twisted corpses lay. The cage offered a partial screening from the cliff top viewers and the pair could approach unobserved.

The three corpses showed no signs of wounds to their bodies; their eyes were bulging, and some saliva or vomit trickled from their open mouths, otherwise nothing else suggested a violent demise.

'What do you think killed these poor men, Dromas? I've seen the death that the plague brings, and death that the failed heart produces, but nothing like this, and why in a cage?'

Looking closer into the cage Dromas sucked in his breath, the air whistling over his teeth. 'Move away, Zenobia! Look at that glass shattered by the cage bars and the wetness of the ground there. They've been poisoned, we best keep back, it may still be effective.'

Zenobia drew back to Dromas's side. 'How horrible, caged and poisoned like rats in a trap! It is an evil thing. I always tried to persuade those we caught to join us and live the life of a free man rather than a slave to the Citadel. If they refused we took their life swiftly, thankfully most chose life.'

Dromas looked appraisingly at Zenobia. 'Is that why you took a chance with me, Zenobia, back in the Landy with half a mountain on top of me?'

Zenobia moved further from the cage to rest in the shadow of a small stand of trees before answering Dromas. 'Back there in the cave, Dromas, another force was at work within me, something that prompted me to save you and I am glad of it. I have been set free. I'm not like those poor souls trapped in that cage, by forgiving you I have stepped away from my imprisoning past.'

'I thank my stars and my instincts that trusted you, Zenobia, not least so I can be here to help you. This weapon they have is only of use if you can get close enough to the enemy to deliver it? Get enough in a closed environment and it would be devastating.'

'That's it!' Gripping Dromas fiercely, Zenobia saw in a flash the horror that Dan planned. 'It's mass murder! It's the end of days. The Tewahedo speak of the prophesy that says a remnant of the Elect must be brought into enlightenment before the pain and suffering of the world can be ended. They must come! The Citadel, it is the last gathering of the Elect, there are no others. Through the ages millions have died. Slaughtered because if they are all gone the prophesy cannot be fulfilled. It is the work of a great evil. A remnant must come here, their homecoming will be the revelation of the end of days and the dawning of something wondrously renewed. Dan is out to destroy humanity's only hope, just as Enoch prophesied, we must stop him!'

Sergeant Dromas of the Borderlands Force and Zenobia, exiled leader from the Great Heights entered the Borderlands intent on travel to the Citadel fired by the vision of horror and hope laid before Zenobia by the Tewahedo. The two rode astride Zenobia's horse, who had been delighted to be reunited with his master, tolerating the additional burden of the sergeant for the pleasure of Zenobia's horsemanship, the only one to whom he would yield.

46

Frumentus's face, flushed from speaking, seemed to glow brighter as he relived the experience of the Paradise. The gathered Elect were transfixed by the account that Frumentus the Fool had thus far given. When they saw his appearance alter, some were stirred deeply as if their life was responding to life. 'Hanok never came back from his meeting, he passed from life. Do not be sad, citizens, at least not for Hanok; he had quested for another understanding of life and he found it. He was right! Endless life is not our true destiny or purpose. He found that our medication is failing, the proof hidden! I've experienced this life, I know it is real! Believe me.'

The Elect grew restless; could it possibly be true? Sensing their unease Frumentus pressed on quickly. 'The life of Hanok has ended, it was but a shadow of the one he is even now beginning to experience. Not endless life, but eternal life! This life is not just lived outside of time, it has a quality that is of a richer dimension than we can possible aspire to here. This book describes that life. It also describes death. Horrible forces that we are encountering, the rise of the Nephilim, of chaos and fire. Armies will gather for a final conflict on the very plains where we now rest. Citizens look around you! Forces of east and west are set to collide, before our eyes friend and foe will clash as the warriors of the Great Heights descend seeking vengeance. We must speak peace to them, avert the clash of nations. Before they come to us let us go to them!'

The unease amongst the Elect grew as Frumentus spoke, as some saw the wisdom of his words while others were sceptical. Voices rose in animated conversation. 'Surely we are safe here.'

'The west will protect us, it always does.'

'Surely the Citadel will rise again?'

'No. Listen to him, look at him. Things are broken. He has changed. So much has happened, it could be right what he says. I just don't know.'

'What would you have us do?' The shout was soon taken up by others. Frumentus pleaded with them, 'Save yourselves from the coming destruction! Come with me! Let us go to the Great Heights and let us make peace with them there. Listen to the words of Enoch and believe!'

The passionate words of this new Frumentus made an impression on some of the gathered but not enough to move them. Davidson roused himself, 'Thank you, Frumentus, for your report. I don't think now is the time for a lengthy recital, there is so much to take in from what you have already said. The safest place for us is here, within the security of the Great Hall pending the arrival of our friends in the west.'

Frumentus slumped into himself, weary from the oration. He had tried his best but other duties called him, and he needed to gain access to Hanok's library. He spoke quietly to Davidson with a renewed energy. 'Sir, if I may return the writings to Hanok's study, it was his wish. I believe there may be other things of interest in there that we need to know.'

Before departing Frumentus looked out over the restless crowd, saddened that they would never come with him. Endlessly perpetuating life that was no life and fearful of the dark. As he looked over the crowd Hanok's voice again entered his mind:

And I said to the man who stood at the gate of the year: "Give me a light that I may tread safely into the unknown." And he replied: "Go out into the darkness and put your hand into the Hand of God. That shall be to you better than light and safer than a known way." So I went forth, and finding the Hand of God, trod gladly into the night.

Frumentus turned and left. Tears in his eyes, he headed for Hanok's library, his footfall echoing through the near silent complex. He travelled into the unknown, his hand firmly in the hand of God; he despaired at events, they simply refused to listen. He had failed.

The library was unlocked and rather shabby. The great mounds of papers and shelves of books seemed to welcome his return, perhaps eager to be explored. 'Where to begin? I have absolutely no idea.' Random lists of words came before Frumentus's eyes. 'Satan Stranger, Sin Shame, Sodomite Suffering... ' the words rolled on.

'Oh, Hanok! How I could use you now.' Frumentus felt a great pressure to find the library of sixty-six. After an aimless shifting of papers Frumentus sat heavily on Hanok's chair, despairing of finding anything. The chair was rather comfortable and the achingly weary Frumentus was drawn towards the blissful arms of Morpheus as he surrendered to the dream of Paradise. He was with Hanok once more, his friend smiling at him, holding a small book bound in leather whilst seated on this very chair. Frumentus smiled back and although he could hear nothing that Hanok said, he was certain something of importance was being conveyed. Hanok finished speaking and seemed to grow somewhat sleepy; the book held in his right hand fell away to his side, slipping in between the seat and arm of the chair as Hanok slept peacefully, untroubled by dreams.

In an instant, Frumentus was awake, and he thrust his hands down the side of the chair to discover the book of his dream. 'It slipped from his hand as it slipped from his mind,' Frumentus marvelled, and opening the front cover discovered a list of sixty-six books was contained in the one library of books. '*Ah yes a "library of sixty-six"; "biblios" in the Greek – we call it the Bible, lots of words in there that guide you to this life that is eternal, read them.*'

Hanok's sleepy voice floated away to leave Frumentus holding the precious words in his hands. He allowed the book to fall open to what looked like well-thumbed pages with many sentences underlined or notated, and one caught his eye. 'I am the resurrection and the life, he who believes in me though he dies yet shall he live and anyone who lives and believes in me shall never die. Do you believe this?'

For reasons unknown Frumentus rather thought he did believe, the vividness of the dream, the way of the invitation to believe, the experience of Paradise coinciding to lead to this conviction. As he turned from underlining to underlining, he saw the book was rich in promises of life and blessings. Surely this was the source of Hanok's quest, much of what he said echoed through the pages. Frumentus knew that these promises and proclamations needed to be heard. Swiftly, he pocketed the book, and headed back towards the Great Hall.

As he turned the last corridor in his approach the pressure wave knocked him forcefully off his feet, and this was followed seconds later by the sound of an enormous explosion. Dazed and confused, Frumentus staggered to his feet amidst the cacophony of warning alarms sounding and sprinklers deploying. He saw the enormous blast doors automatically closing, designed as they were to seal the inhabitants of the Great Hall from the peril of the nuclear blast. In that safe space the population would breathe filtered air and draw upon stored supplies that would sustain them until the contamination passed.

Situated above the roof of the hall, the last of the cylinders was unscrewed onto a weakened thread that would briefly withstand the pressure of the gas before yielding. As the thread failed the cap blasted away, leaving the contents to pour out. Drawn and carried by the filtered air supply, it was silently pumped into the hall. The place of safety became a vast gas chamber.

Frumentus staggered towards the doors but by the time he reached them they had firmly clicked shut; he turned to rest his back against them, slowly sliding down onto the floor and into unconsciousness.

47

Mercifully, their swift travel had not lasted long. Zenobia's horse wasn't able to sustain the considerable extra weight and the pair had resorted to walking as fast as Dromas's still healing injuries allowed, the horse set free to return to the Heights. As veterans of the Borderlands they had sensed the coming windstorm long before it broke over them, so the sudden furious lashing of wind whipped sand was avoided as they huddled in a rocky crevice. It was this storm that saved them from the nuclear blast.

Far out in the plain of Megiddo the converging forces had no shelter. Caught in the sand storm the warriors of the Great Heights huddled, cloaks thrown over their heads, well prepared for the coming storm. Blind without drones to guide them, the rescue battalion from the east crashed straight into them. In near blind conditions, each fought vicious hand-to-hand combat, stabbing and slicing at close quarter, sophisticated weaponry useless as the fighting raged as furious as the storm.

Samyaza watched gleefully as a third force crashed into the melee, drawn into conflict as the forces of the Citadel attacked. All around was the wonderful sight of human beings killing each other. For Samyaza it was the richest pleasure.

Reluctantly, he contacted Turiel, for as much as he enjoyed witnessing humans tearing at themselves it was time for the tactical nuclear weapons to be detonated. Taking a last look at the chaos, he withdrew into the darkness underground and gave the order. A series of massive explosions convulsed the land as the warheads exploded simultaneously, the shockwave rolling through the earth and the sky. Samyaza was confident no one would have survived the blast, but he denied himself the pleasure of viewing the carnage as he led the Watchers towards the Citadel.

Zenobia and Dromas were shaken by the blast but shielded from its devastating force by the rock. Dromas knew better than to venture out as he waited for the second blast and firestorm to sweep by. The pair resumed their journey through a now devastated landscape, skirting the edge of the site of battle where nothing lived. Zenobia was unable to comprehend the scale of destruction that lay scattered across the plain, it was truly an appalling sight. Blackened corpses lay fallen in battle, friend and foe bound together. Zenobia wept at the sight of those friends she could identify, lost in an instant of madness.

'Zenobia, we're as dead as they are, there's a fallout that follows the fire and it brings death, just at a slower pace.' Dromas moved slowly amongst the burned out Landies where colleagues and friends who had once laughed and sworn and fought, now lay silent.

Zenobia was numb to his words at first but eventually their meaning penetrated her mind. 'What destruction has been brought to us. Truly it is the end of days.'

They were glad to leave behind the carnage as they approached the Citadel. Remarkably the blast had not thrown it to the ground, it remained held drunkenly unguarded in its cradle. Silence reigned within. Whilst the blast-wave had inflicted yet more damage on the structure, it was easy enough to pick a way through towards the Great Hall where Dromas expected to find his people sheltered by the blast doors. He hoped that the communications systems would still function but as he surveyed the debris his confidence levels were sinking.

They found Frumentus's slumped body in front of the doors, for all the world he seemed to be dead. Zenobia's heart raced frantically as she rushed to his side. 'He's still with us, Dromas, the blast can't have been so devastating in here.' Gently, they tended to the unconscious Frumentus, and having satisfied themselves that it was safe, they moved him away from the doors to a sheltered spot.

Frumentus lay still whilst Zenobia moistened his lips with water, speaking tenderly to him. 'Frumentus, come back to me. Frumentus, I need you with me, so much has befallen us. Such suffering and sorrow lies behind us. Now I think suffering will be forever before us. These people must come with us back to the Paradise in the Heights. Did they listen to you, Frumentus, or did they shut these doors in your face?'

In the howling desert Frumentus heard a child crying. 'Help me, I'm lost, please help me.' He staggered in shredded clothes towards the sound of the cries, eventually coming to a small child standing alone and calling for help.

'Don't worry, I'm here with you, I won't fail you, come to me.'

The child looked up with soulful eyes. 'Save us, help us, we're all lost, we can't breathe, can't swallow. Everything is squeezing us, beating us, hating us.' The child turned and pointed where spread out on a vast plain were thousands of children crying for help. 'Save us, we're lost, it's so cold here, I'm scared, please you can save us, you can help us, please will you? We're sorry, please don't let us be punished anymore; we didn't know!'

The anguish rose as a wind picked up the swirling sand to a new intensity, stinging the eyes and the flesh, obscuring the multitude, but their voices stayed with Frumentus. How could he reach them, how could he save them? He plunged into the sandstorm, searching for them, hearing their desperate cries now here, now there, he turned this way and that, but he just couldn't reach them. He cried out in his own anguish as the words from the bible came to him. 'Do you believe this…?'

'I believe this, I believe this! Please, I don't want them to be lost. I don't want them to suffer alone. Help me reach them! Let me just hold them and comfort them. Oh please help me!'

The storm stilled, the children were gone, their footprints erased, and there stood Zenobia in radiant splendour. 'I've come for you, Frumentus, my Frumentus, to bring you back. Don't stay here looking for the lost ones, we can't yet help them, come back to me.' Drawing close to him she reached up on her toes and kissed him, leaving her moisture on his dried and cracked lips. Frumentus looked around in vain for any signs of the children and finding none placed his hands in hers and walked into the darkness, unafraid.

'Quiet!' hissed Dromas, 'someone is coming.' Frumentus had struggled back to consciousness and was babbling over the sight of Zenobia who sat with him trying to bathe his various cuts and bruises.

'They're alive! Oh that's wonderful.' Zenobia was thrilled at the prospect that others had survived beyond the protection of the blast doors.

'Be still, Zenobia, and shut him up. We've no idea who is out there, friend or foe. We lie low until we can work them out.' Dromas had heard the sound of many feet padding along towards the blast doors just in time to allow Zenobia, Frumentus and himself to bury themselves into the dark corner of the shelter. From their place of concealment they saw the shadowy party approach, and after much effort prise open the vast doors sufficiently for the figures to slip one by one into the Great Hall, disappearing from view.

'Dromas, do you think they are a rescue squad, should we follow them?' Zenobia was uneasy at the sight of the party, something about them seemed wrong and it made the hairs on her neck rise, a primeval response to a threat as yet unknown. Soon they reappeared with five inert forms carried on their shoulders.

Wordlessly the group padded away.

After a considerable wait Dromas eased his way out from under the hiding place and slunk cautiously over the blast doors. Satisfied that he was alone, he slipped through into the Great Hall. As they waited Frumentus and Zenobia spoke quietly of events that had taken place.

'Perhaps the Elect will at last listen to you, Frumentus, after this latest attack upon them, they must now see the peril they face and the hope we can offer.'

'You won't save them. They're dead, all of them, thousands gone.' Dromas spoke in a flat monotone. 'Nowhere to run, nowhere to hide, you were right. An entire race, my people, wiped out.'

Such epic destruction broke the mind of Dromas; memories of the horrors of the burning settlements flew at him, demons from the past joining the grotesque present with tormenting screams and accusations. 'I don't think I can take this sorrow anymore, Zenobia, you said if we can't rescue a remnant here and bring them back the end will never come. All this hatred and butchery will spin on endlessly as we tear ourselves to pieces. Where is the justice in this? Where the judgement of evil, this is all so unfair.'

Frumentus rose unsteadily to his feet, made his way over to the doors and entered. It was as Dromas had said an awful sight. The gas had dispersed evenly across the hall. People must have come to a realisation that death had come. People had started tearing at the doors to try and get out. Piles of bodies lay by the exits which bore the marks of frantic attempts to smash them down. Others lay calmly in the arms of their partners, elsewhere individuals turned in on themselves smashing their heads against the floor to try and bring the suffering to an earlier end.

There was no dignity here, no respect of the fact that these were the Elect who had for so long soared above other people, secure in their science, insulated against the ravages of time. *'Oh Citadel,*

Citadel if only you had listened, how I longed to gather you under my wings, but you would not.' Hanok's lament became Frumentus's as he gazed mutely out over a sea of death.

He turned as he felt Zenobia's hand reach his. 'Come on, Frumentus, we can't help them now, come away with me.' Painfully he allowed himself to be led away from the Great Hall to where Dromas stood. Frumentus had no words of consolation or encouragement for this broken man, he simply embraced him. There the two men of the Citadel stood held in a wordless embrace as they wept for the nation that was now lost.

48

Dan had chosen his men well. They were natural born killers, easily persuaded of the justness of their cause. Each had a deep-rooted bitterness towards the Citadel and all it represented. In each the desire for vengeance was all-consuming. Dan held them in a grip of malice that drove them on their destructive course. Together they had placed the cylinders above the vast ceiling of the Great Hall. Silently the caps of the cylinders were unscrewed, the final turn onto the weakened thread made when the nuclear blast was heard. He was pleased with the resulting death, losing only one of the riders, the cylinder malfunctioning bursting its cap prematurely. All the others were out of the Citadel, swiftly heading away from the scene of carnage to join the Watchers in their lair to await the all clear when once the nerve agent filtered out of the chamber, corpses of the ambassador's staff were to be gathered to lay a trail back to the sanctuary at the Great Heights for the vengeful to follow. Now with the corpses strapped to the horses Dan headed away from the Citadel, taking a large detour south away from the carnage to avoid detection. The sky was filling with drones and the sound of mechanised infantry and tank battalions could be heard. The riders veered away out into the Borderlands, travelling cautiously mainly at night.

49

'What did Dromas mean, Zenobia, when he spoke of the remnant needing to return with us?' Frumentus asked. 'Does this atrocity ripple yet further out to damage others?' Tired and worn down, the three sat closely together in Hanok's library, the books oddly comforting.

Zenobia heard again the sonorous voice reading. '*A remnant will return to the Mighty God. Though your people be like the sand by the sea, only a remnant will return. Then the destruction that has been decreed, overwhelming and righteous will come. The Almighty will carry out the destruction decreed upon the whole land then the deliverer will come, he will turn godlessness away, it is he who will come as judge to destroy evil and usher in goodness.*'

Frumentus saw the sadness in Zenobia's face as she recalled the words, her voice weary when she spoke again. 'I am told that if the Elect do not return then evil can't be judged and suffering ended. Everything depended on their return. Now they've been murdered, how can they return? All is lost. Evil finally achieved what it always desired. It has been determined to wipe out your people, to prevent such a return ever happening, throughout the history of the world. Never have a people been so persecuted. Now whatever this evil is, it has succeeded. These tens of thousands of dead were all that remained, the descendants of the earthquake survivors, themselves survivors of the death camps and the pogroms now all gone.'

Frumentus saw that this spirit of deep despair had gripped Dromas as well as Zenobia; the loss of life was an act of evil malice with consequences that boded ill for the rest of humanity. Frumentus could only guess at the ramifications of a nuclear attack, combined with the slaughter of civilians, the panic and blame at the loss of precious life-extending chemicals, senseless death and apportionment of blame.

'This can only escalate, Zenobia, the superpowers will find it hard to restrain the hawks in their ranks from retaliation for these attacks, the prophecy is being fulfilled. Truly evil is coming and we can't hope to stop it.' As he spoke, Frumentus was touched by the awful truth of his words. He was a fool to think he could have made any difference or been of any help to the Citadel. As his mind began to grow numb with despair, his hands took on a life of their own, patting his pockets they felt for the Hanok's bible. Picking it up, he allowed it to fall open.

Listlessly, fingers turned the well-thumbed pages until they stopped at some underlined and annotated words. '*The coming of the lawless one will be in accordance with the work of Satan, displayed in all kinds of counterfeit miracles, signs and wonders, and in every sort of evil that deceives those who are perishing. They perish because they refused to love the truth and so be saved.*' By the side of the text, written presumably in Hanok's own writing, were the words "Dan & the Citadel?!"

'Zenobia, look at this!' He read the verse and the notation. 'Zenobia, the lawless one, the worker of signs and wonders, the deceiver, it's Dan. Those that wouldn't listen, that's the Citadel The coldness that Hanok saw growing in his soul can only have been the growing of what was already lying there, perhaps a dormant seed of evil awaiting the call to life. In the darkness of that chamber! That's when the call came. After that time he was lost to us!'

Zenobia now pieced other aspects of the story together, a conviction growing within her. 'When I sought him in the healing place there was another presence there, a stranger I could not see.'

Frumentus sprang up at Zenobia's words. He rushed to the paperwork he had first read through on his arrival. Grabbing it, he brought it to Zenobia. 'Look at the words, Zenobia, *Satan Stranger, Sin Shame, Sodomite Suffering,* is it a coincidence that the words *"Satan" and* "*Stranger*" are grouped together? Did Hanok know or at least suspect that there was more to Dan than first met the eye, was there something strange about him? Maybe that is why he hid the bible from Dan. Could it unmask who he really is and what forces are behind him?

'My people, I am ashamed of the destruction they have brought, now here "*sin*" and "*shame*" are another pair. The Elect have shamefully brought suffering to your land, that's a surely a sin.

'Now look here at the account back here where it talks about Sodom and Gomorrah. They refused to offer a welcome to God's messengers, seeking to rape them instead. They suffered a rain of fire, see Hanok's notes. *My people rape the land, they drive away with hatred.* Did he really see the future of our time contained in this book?'

Zenobia puzzled over the story. 'From his notation I would say he was concerned that no one listened to his warnings. They rejected the messenger and brutalised his character.' Her energy levels draining, Zenobia sighed, deep in frustration and regret at all that had occurred. 'If only they had listened, maybe all this pain would have been avoided.'

Dromas was unmoved by the excitement that gripped the others, and he stared bleakly into Frumentus's face. 'Fool! They didn't listen to you and they are dead. All of them! Couldn't you have tried harder to warn them? Said something; anything, to get through to them? You failed them and they're dead. There is no Elect, no Remnant.

They lie dead in the Great Hall all of them. We're lost in this hell forever, trapped in this soulless home alone, the living dead!'

Frumentus stared at Dromas as each word pierced him, nailing him to a shame he would carry all the days of his life. The sin and shame of failure was his. Frumentus stared out into the darkness of a future without hope, where evil and suffering would reign unchecked and all that was good would be destroyed. He had tasted the life that could have been in Paradise, a vivid, beautifully animated reality. In comparison the suffering and slaughter that had come to pass was a profound sadness and crippling shame for Frumentus to be buried; hidden away, for that was the lot of Frumentus the Fool.

Into such darkness a light flickered and a far distant voice whispered, reaching to Frumentus in his darkest moments. 'Of course!' he cried. 'Yes of course, that's it *Sin Shame*, hidden away! The Remnant, Zenobia, that's it! They're hidden away. The shameful failures of the Corporation, the ones who know the truth that endless life is a lie. They're in the Homes, Zenobia! The remnant are in the Homes that Hanok spoke of!'

Zenobia came sharply out of her reverie. 'The Homes, of course the Homes! How many are there? How many do they hold? Where are they?' Words tumbled out of her mouth as hope flickered into life once again.

'I'm not sure of the total number, but Hanok spoke of several homes and told me how to find one of them.'

'Dromas, Sergeant Dromas!' Zenobia reached over to the inert form. 'Did you hear what Frumentus said? There are others that could still be alive that we can help, please, Dromas, don't give up.'

Dromas roused himself, looking at Zenobia with confused and angry eyes. He spat out his pain. 'What's the point eh! A few fragile creatures can make no difference.'

'Oh, Dromas, we don't know that, anything is possible with God.'

Dromas's anger flared at such talk. 'Don't talk to me of God! How can a god allow this to happen? I heard such talk amongst the mercenaries and other simple folk. They say God is all powerful and all loving so why allow this horror? It's just a lie told to children. God can't be all loving or he would have stopped this, or if He is loving but is unable to stop it He can't be all powerful can He? So why do you think bringing a few frail failures to the Great Heights can possibly change all this? He spared none when the earthquakes came, entire cities lost to destruction, pestilence killing thousands who had the misfortune to survive the quake, my people gave up on God after that, we are our own saviours these days! Free, floating over an unstable world.'

Zenobia withdrew her hand from his shoulder, burnt by the heat of his passion. 'Dromas, God is love. I now know that. I've felt that love. God didn't kill these people, evil killed them. That's what happens when love is rejected; evil grows, spurred on by malignant beings. We are all free to choose, to pursue the way of love or to reject it and so fall into evil as Dan has. God is love and love has to take a risk that it will be rejected. You cannot force someone to love you, it is a free choice and it is a real choice that has real consequences. That is where our dignity as human beings comes from. He offers us His love and allows us to accept or reject it. Suffering and sorrow stem from people who turn away from love. I don't understand how bringing a Remnant to the Great Heights fits into the great scheme of things, but I believe what I have heard.'

Seeing some flicker of life spark in the sergeant's eyes, Zenobia pressed on urgently. 'Dromas, I can understand your sorrow and anguish at what you have seen today. I don't speak as one who has never tasted the bitter pain of loss, you know that. All I hope and trust is that the goodness of a loving God will eventually make sense of all that has been. One day everything in this broken world will be taken up into His loving purposes and refashioned in a glorious renewal. It is this renewal that awaits the return of at least some of the Elect. They are the original people to whom God made His solemn agreement. Even if you don't believe any of what I have said, surely you can see how cruel it would be to leave people, your people, alone in the wilderness to perish? Come on, Dromas, please help us in this.'

50

The two Landies raced over the barren land, both towing pairs of long trailers, Frumentus leading the way. Zenobia's passion had broken through to Dromas. A grim determination had settled upon him as he steered the vehicle in the dust trail that was being thrown up. As the miles passed, his grip eased on the wheel. 'You can't beat these Landies you know, chuck any challenge at them or even a nuclear bomb and they'll still try for you!'

They had been fortunate to find some vehicles sheltered from the blast. These had been used primarily for transporting building materials and equipment for the repair of the Citadel, and their work completed they had been abandoned at some distance to the rear of the security perimeter. Each was attached to its primary trailer and capable of hooking a further dolly behind. With luck these could transport several hundred patients at a time, albeit squashed together and travelling slowly.

Now there was no slowness of travel, just a vast cloud of dust thrown up by Frumentus's frantic pace. It had occurred to all three that if they had realised the importance the occupants of the Homes now held, others could have as well. Frumentus was confident of Hanok's directions which had been quite precisely given, as if he knew there would be a need for Frumentus to go there. *'Who are you, Hanok, really? What did you know about Dan, the Watchers and all the rest?*' Time was too pressing for Frumentus to dwell on such thoughts. They needed to reach the first Home and recover the people there and move on to the next. Frumentus hoped that there would be some clue to the location of the other Homes in this first one, which was the distinct impression he had from Hanok.

Within a few hours' travel they reached the same low building Shylock had encountered in his search for Marcus. The vehicles pulled up in a cloud of dust. Frumentus tried the intercom to no avail and so resorted to ramming the gates with the Landy, and wrenching the front doors off the main entrance by hooking a wire hawser through the handles and onto the front-mounted winch.

Once inside it became apparent that the order for all synths to return to their docking stations had been transmitted to the home. The stench was overpowering as patients struggled to help others incapable of caring for their own toileting needs. Many lay motionless in their beds, others on the floors where they had fallen, unable to rise.

Horrified at the scene of such frailty and suffering amongst his own people, Dromas was desperate to help. 'Can we reactivate the synths, Frumentus?' Moving to help the most mobile of the residents, Dromas worked swiftly, calming and reassuring them that they were to be taken to a better place. 'If we can it would speed up our work here, they can carry the inert onto the trailers whilst the others walk there. It's got to be worth the risk of malfunction!'

Frumentus stared at the control panel of the reception desk; dare they reawaken the synths? He knew he could but what would happen if he did? Caught in indecision, his eye fell on some clear directions to another Home. He moved to override the docking command and was relieved to see the carers reanimate and as he was Head of Security, respond to his command to assist in the loading.

With all loaded the passenger tally was nearly two hundred. Not all would travel well but it was agreed that none should be left behind. The journey to the next Home was far slower, but within the hour events repeated themselves and they moved towards the third, further directions emerging from Home to Home.

'We've nearly filled the trailers, Dromas; I hope they can endure the travelling, so many of them are frail. It's hard to imagine what life must have been like for them in those places, anything we do must be better than this.' Dromas had to agree, at last they seemed to be making a positive difference rather than simply chasing a trail of destruction, and he fervently hoped the tide was now turning in their favour. When they reached the sixth Home with the vehicles dangerously loaded it became apparent that the tide was running entirely the other way.

Here there was evidence of violent death strewn across the complex. Residents had died by the blade, some going quietly into the dark night whilst others raged at the dying of the light, but their struggles were in vain. 'This Home is the furthest from the Citadel, closest to the western border, our trail has run cold. It is most likely to be on the path of the advancing forces. With this knife work it points a bloody finger at the warriors from the Great Heights. Even now we are pursued.' Frumentus pointed to a small but ominously growing dust cloud heading in their direction.

51

The Landies went as fast as they dared across the plain heading for the Great Heights, and behind them, judging from the evidence of the dust cloud, their pursuers were gaining on them which was no surprise. 'How long before nightfall do you think, Zenobia? I'm thinking darkness is going to be our best hope.'

'You're right, Dromas, it'll fall fast when it comes. I'm guessing another half hour or so. We must go carefully, we don't want to lose Frumentus whilst shaking them off our tail. We're close to the site of the ambush that brought us together. If we can get there, we will find a whole maze of dried river beds and pass through unseen.'

Signalling to Frumentus, they diverted their course from a straight run to the Great Heights and reached the network of wadis as night fell. Once the moon was sufficiently bright they made their cautious way along the beds, the slower speed a relief to those on the trailers. Turning to check the state of the many passengers, Dromas slowed the vehicle.

'They're bouncing around in the back, I'm afraid. I doubt the weakest will survive much more of this. Ironic that the places where these folk came from were called "homes", I'd say they were prisons or dumping grounds. If how you treat your frail and ageing is a measure of a society then we were pretty much broken even before we fell from the sky.'

Zenobia nodded. 'A community of love cares for young and old, weak and vulnerable; it's all about giving of your strength to help the weak, we see it as love in action.'

Dromas snorted. 'Zenobia, you speak a lot about love and I'm guessing you're after bringing me into the family of your god. I wouldn't fit in your world, I've killed too many of your people, how could I possibly live with them? You saved my life and you tell me you did so because you wanted better for me and I am forever indebted to you for that. You forgave me all that pain, Zenobia, when by rights you could have taken my life. To be honest it crushes me, I can't repay you for all you have done, and I can't bring back the lives taken. I'm simply not worthy.'

Silence fell as the two stared out at the ground of the winding river bed that the Landy was slowly eating up. 'It's a gift, Dromas. You don't have to be worthy to receive a gift, you just have to be loved by the giver and humble enough to receive that which is given. You tell me the effect of the radiation is fatal for us, come home with me, don't be alone in these last days.'

The Landy rumbled on in silence, the invitation hanging in the air. Eventually the convoy left the river-bed, when cresting the bank they saw the road snaking up to the summit ahead.

Dromas frowned at the route. 'There's no way we can drive all the way up that with these double trailers attached. We can make the first turn in the road then, we'll have to uncouple and load the sickest into the vehicles and get the others to climb up, some of them are still strong enough to help, I think. Let's get there then we'll let Frumentus know the plan.'

As the sun rose the vehicles cast long shadows across the plain; the journey had gone better than they could have hoped. There was no sign of the dust cloud behind them and the way ahead was clear. The distant sound of heavy machinery moving could be heard and the sky was crisscrossed with vapour trails, so clearly things were stirring, as forces were set to collide.

The sooner we're up and away from this, the better, Zenobia thought. She wondered if the news of the destruction had reached people here. She knew the devastation it would bring to families and hoped they would still offer hospitality. It would be hard for anyone to see these frail frightened people as enemies to be hated when they were all caught up in the same destructive storm, victims of forces beyond their control.

With the vehicles stopped, the work of moving the weakest began whilst others began to climb the road on foot. Zenobia's eyes swept the plain constantly, her instincts telling her something dangerous was coming. For a while she saw nothing but as the sun rose higher she saw it, the cloud of dust was heading directly for them at speed.

'Dromas, Frumentus, quickly, move them quickly! Our pursuers are coming!' Both men saw the danger and urged the people forward. Now all were climbing the steeping road, and the Landies were loaded ready to ascend. 'They'll soon catch up with us, Zenobia! I've an idea that we can slow them by blocking the road with the trailers. They're no use to us now so let's launch them back down the road to crush those who climb after us.'

The pursuers were clearly visible to Zenobia. 'It's Dan leading the horsemen, they're riding hard! I bet it was these who slaughtered the people in the home. I recognise some who ride with him!' Zenobia counted ten horsemen she knew instinctively they were coming to wipe out the Remnant before they could climb to safety.

'We must stop them! Dromas, do what you can with the trailers. I'm going to prepare another surprise for them!' She left, running swiftly towards a large fissure in the base of the rock face, whistling up her horse who had again made its own way back from the Citadel. It snickered, pleased to see its mistress as it emerged from the fissure, stroking its muzzle Zenobia spoke quietly to it before leading it back into the stable to await the time of ambush.

52

The discovery of the home was accidental; lights shining in the darkness led them to it. Slaughtering all inside had been a swift bloody affair. Dan could find little information about the place and with time pressing he simply left one of the corpses from the Citadel nearby, ensuring the trail from the Home would be obvious for anyone to spot, then he rode straight for the Great Heights dropping corpses along the way.

Now Dan was furious to see so many people ascending the road to safety. The Master wanted all from the Citadel killed. Dan didn't care why they had to die, he feared failing his Master. He urged his riders on, in his fury lashing his tired horse onwards to close in on their prey. He could see the Landies slowly climbing the first of a series of steep inclines, dragging cumbersome trailers, clearly struggling to make progress. As they drew closer scores of people could be seen clambering off the now stationary convoy, climbing the steep road as fast as they could at the sight of death galloping towards them. His riders were outpacing Dan, seeing their homeland being assaulted by the hated enemy drove them recklessly forward.

Soon they were climbing the road themselves, partially blinded by the dust the vehicles had thrown up as they strained forward. The first five riders had no way of avoiding one of the unhitched trailers that came hurtling out of the dust as it careered back down the hill. It smashed into them, shattering the limbs of rider and horse alike before crashing into the rock at the bottom of the road. Others further down the road had time to turn their horses and avoid the onrushing trailer. When the second trailer was launched it hit the bodies of the fallen and flew into the air, where twisting wildly it shattered as it hit the cliff face at great speed, sending shards of metal and wood into the second group of horsemen.

The survivors from this assault turned and fled to the base to regroup, preferring to face Dan's fury. As the horses pranced nervously, refusing to come under control, Zenobia charged through them wielding a light sabre, slashing the throat of the closest rider before bursting clear of the group on the other side. Her horse, far fresher than their mounts, spun around and plunged back into the confusion. Zenobia ducked a blade thrust before back-chopping its owner, severing his spinal cord at the neck.

Three riders remained with Dan, all carrying heavy swords and one a lance. Zenobia was outmatched. She turned and raced for the road, leaping the fallen debris. The lancer raced after her, his larger mount clearing the debris with ease and eating the ground up, the lance tip inches from Zenobia's exposed spine. As he drew back his arm to make a killing thrust he was knocked violently sideways. He flew from his horse as Dromas landed heavily on him, knocking both horse and rider into a wall of stone that was the edge of the road.

Dromas's leap had been from a height and the landing opened the wound in his chest, but he managed to stand and confront the rider who was struggling to free his feet from the fallen horse. As he kicked free he rose, sword in hand, to lunge at Dromas. The sword pierced Dromas's side, glancing his ribs as he tried to twist away from the thrust. The sword came again but this time it made no contact as a well-aimed rock cracked the skull of the swordsman, rendering him unconscious. Dromas turned blearily to see Zenobia dismounting and running towards him armed with two more rocks and her slingshot ready to launch at the prone figure if required.

'They never look up, Dromas, do they, you brave man! Thank you for saving my life.' Dromas reached for her as his vision blurred and he sank to his knees, the tip of a sword emerging from his stomach. He fell to reveal Dan standing holding the bloodied blade.

'You're causing me a lot of trouble today, you little bitch! You're supposed to be locked away in your safe house awaiting my pleasure.'

A rock smashed into Dan's teeth, sending him to the ground. 'You lie. Evil grips you. Only Spiro saved me from rape!'

Spitting blood and teeth, Dan's words sprayed from his broken mouth. 'Your Spiro couldn't protect you! Master snapped his neck like a twig. He wants me to have you. And I will!' Turning to his surviving troop Dan snarled, 'Get her!'

The remaining two riders hesitated before backing away from Zenobia, the spell broken by the truth of Spiro's death and Zenobia's innocence.

Dan struggled to his feet mopping the blood. 'Cowards!' he screamed. 'I'll do it myself.' He advanced towards Zenobia, who had dropped her slingshot and drawn her light sabre. It was no match in strength to Dan's blade, but she had the speed and agility to avoid his heavy cuts. Soon Dan was panting heavily as he swung and missed repeatedly. She backed him against the rock wall where Zenobia's blade sliced his arms and thighs, blood free flowing from many lacerations.

Dan stopped trying to raise the sword to strike the girl and for a moment his eyes cleared, and he saw her before him, as if for the first time. Then came the voice again. '*Do you see her? Look. Is she not wondrous? We watch them, we see them, we know them, we desire them. Open your eyes, look, are they not... gorgeous; are you not engorged?*' Dan shook his head, trying to clear away the insistent voice weakening by the second. The blade dropped to the floor. 'I see her, I truly see her, she's lovely.'

Zenobia stepped towards Dan who had slumped into unconsciousness. 'Dan, come back to us, please, Dan.'

'It's Daniel actually!' Animated by another power, Dan was on his feet in an instance, sword whirling in his hand, striking at the crouching Zenobia. Her rising blade was too slow to catch the downward strike, but her catlike instincts saw her twist away from its reach. Now unarmed, Zenobia faced the power of the one possessing Dan.

'"Daniel", far more dignified, don't you think, Zenobia? I've been watching you, Zenobia, for a long time, waiting to see which way you would go. I did what I could to persuade you. Your parents... such a shame; those beastly men, how could they? Again, and again and again. I was there waiting for you. The bitch in you never really grew as I wanted and now you're all together, reunited, reconciled. Such a pity, I had high hopes for you.'

The voice wasn't Dan's though his mouth moved, it was an elegant clipped voice that drew her towards the sword. 'Daniel is a disappointment to me, oh what are we to do? They're getting away from me. But the game isn't over yet.'

Zenobia kept backing away from the sword, back towards the wreckage of the trailers as the smooth words continued. High above, the refugees could be seen cresting the heights, safe. Relieved at the sight, Zenobia stumbled, a fallen horse her undoing. The blade snaked in for the kill then faltered and dropped from a hand that reached now to draw out Zenobia's boot knife embedded in his throat. Sobbing for breath, the earth loose beneath her feet, Zenobia scrambled up. The thrown blade had caught Dan in the throat; it wasn't a death blow, but was sufficient in force to cause Dan to sink to his knees.

There was no sound of the other voice to be heard, just the gurgling of blood and the gasping. Dan wrenched the blade out, his eyes bulging in terror at the sightless horror approaching one who disappointed the Master. He fell into darkness. In the corner of her eye Zenobia saw Turiel grasping his own throat, mimicking the agony of Dan's death. 'We's scared, Master is coming. It's so dark and cold, he's coming, he's coming!' The tiny creature curled up into a ball to protect itself from the endless world of pain, the fate of creature and child.

53

The Arabian and African tectonic plates grind against each other in their gradual northerly journey to form the Dead Sea Transform Fault System, one part of the restless world upon which civilization rests. The severity of the grinding of the earth is on one hand a continuation of creation, the formless called into dynamic being, whilst on the other it is the birth pains of a good thing spoiled. Either way, when sufficient energy is amassed the resultant expression of restless rock is devastating. Through the course of history, civilisations and religions have been shaped by the power of the molten earth, whole cities consumed, deities placated. The greatest devastation had swept through the region almost within living memory when the earth split open in a series of shuddering eruptions and earthquakes taking millions of lives, the land washed clean by devastating tsunamis.

It was to avoid such losses recurring that the Elect had harnessed the power of the finest minds with the ruthless determination of a people who were forever fleeing persecution, to create the Citadel that would ride above any future devastation visited on the Promised Land. Huge cost and advanced technology made it possible to float in the troughs of audio waves. The land was unstable, physically and politically and, whilst immune from most convulsions, the Citadel knew it was always a pawn in the great game, their only security the precious knowledge of endless life they held.

As the remnant of the now fallen Citadel climbed the heights seeking to escape Dan's horsemen, such forces were being unleashed once more. Detonation of the nuclear warheads proved to be enough. Tremors reached deep into the unstable fault line, offering vast chambers of molten material an opportunity to push upwards. A violent shaking was stirring into life as east and west clashed. So far the conflict had been contained within the region; however political hawks were pressing the case to strike with overwhelming force.

~ ~ ~

Zenobia eased herself painfully away from the lifeless figure of Dan. Breathing with difficulty she reached the place Dromas where lay, lifeless eyes staring upwards, as if surprised that death had found him at last. Zenobia whistled up her horse and with the help of the remaining horsemen began the task of carrying Dromas to the gates of Paradise. She picked her way carefully through the carnage, eventually cresting the heights with the last of the stragglers from the Citadel.

From this vantage she could see the unfolding drama of two great forces clashing below on the plain. Frumentus joined her, gazing out at the unfolding tragedy. 'Zenobia, we failed to prevent this clash, no one listened and the thousands that have died will be joined by many, many more. We have the Remnant here. Do we take them to the healing place?'

'No, Frumentus, we all go to the Paradise. The prophesy said a Remnant will be gathered in and then the end will come. Gather everyone and meet me there.'

54

As Zenobia approached Paradise she found her way barred by an unmoving figure. She sought to calm the nervous prancing horses, dismounting and keeping a firm grip on the reins and blowing up their nostrils whilst stroking tensed necks. 'That's right, well done, Zenobia, nice and calm now, easy, girl.' The stranger was by her side, calming her with long strokes down her flank his breath in her nose.

'That's better, isn't it? You can let go now if you want.' Entranced, Zenobia eased the grip on the reins, allowing the horses to pull free and race away. She stood alone with the well-groomed stranger who dominated her with his words. 'What are we going to do with you, young Zenobia? You've been such a trouble and now it's just you and me alone in this place. I think we'll need to bring things to an end, our end, Zenobia, yours, mine and that of all humanity.'

He smiled winsomely, cocking his head as he regraded her. 'How sweet that our destinies are so intimately entwined. You, the saviour of the people, whereas I am their destroyer. Together we shall know life lived in exile from our Creator, a living death where no good things exist, only perpetual fear and unending thirst. Constantly at war in your soul, seeking to escape the coldness of the dark but drawing back ashamed at what the light reveals.'

Turning to look over the plain he continued. 'How delightful, human beings ashamed in their nakedness, their darkest deeds and desires laid bare for all to see. Every generation fabricating their own fig leaves in vainglorious attempts to hide their disgusting selves away, allowing only their presentable parts to be seen. You see, your kind were a threat to us, formed to carry the image of your Creator within you, representing Him to the whole earth. My earth, Zenobia! He chose your kind over mine to work together because he saw it was good!'

The controlled pronunciation was slipping as the stranger spoke with increasing agitation, spittle flying from lips that writhed like snakes. 'I came to the first of your kind and showed them another way, knowledge and beauty could be possessed, not simply admired, used powerfully for your own dominance of this planet, not just its stewardship, you could become like Him. He formed you in His image and I gave the chance to return the compliment and form Him in yours. And you took it. The great exile occurred, forever you could have lived, but death was brought to you as a mercy. He was determined you would not endlessly live a life of suffering exile and so you were banished from the Garden. We saw you in your beauty and we desired you. We took you and we created a new race from women and angels in defiance of His will. The Nephilim were beautiful, powerful dominant, made in my image, Zenobia, mine, for I am the prince of this world!'

As he drew close to the trembling girl, the words grew in harshness. 'Daniel carried the line in him. It was awoken by his choice, for he saw all that could be and he desired it! How about you, Zenobia? Will you allow yourself to desire? Will the Nephilim rise in you?'

Zenobia stood motionless, caught in the words of the stranger. They moved away from Paradise, walking towards the cliff edge where laid before them were the clashing armies, beyond them the fallen Citadel and much more. Great cities, innumerable people, food, wealth, all were dazzling to the eye of the beholder.

'Do you see how good it is? Don't you want to taste this life? See,

I set before you life and death, blessing and curses, follow me, Zenobia, and choose life!'

Zenobia remained still as the temptation continued then eventually, as one coming round from a deep sleep, she stirred slowly into life. The stranger stood by her side, his arm upon her shoulder. She looked out again at the splendour laid before her but in her mind's eye she saw the burning fire destroy her parents' love, she felt the weight of many men pressing into her young body, the thousands of faces and forms distorted by death. These were replaced by the smiling faces of Spiro and Dromas and then Frumentus. These images gradually faded from before her eyes to be replaced by that of Hanok and the three, standing waiting for her to come to them as even now the Remnant of the Citadel were flooding into Paradise together with the people of the settlement.

Zenobia knew it was accomplished. She turned to face the stranger who smiled in triumph as Zenobia nodded, decision made. 'I want nothing of your world or your ways!' Zenobia shouted as she twisted out from under his arm and backed away from him rapidly. 'I choose not to seek power over people but to use power to help people. I choose to love, not love to choose what is best for me and if that means I must die, I choose to die to a lifeless way and live for another way!'

Anger swept across the stranger's features, no longer was he a suave and well-dressed picture of elegance. Now his features contorted through a thousand leering faces of hatred, some of the men who had thrust themselves upon her, others the faces of cruel tormentors, despots, heads of corporations, leaders of terror cells, abusive church clergy and endlessly on. Zenobia could no longer stand to see the evil that lay behind so much of the world. She ran at the creature, leaping with feet outstretched. As she landed squarely on his chest, her momentum sent both out over the edge of the cliff to fall to their doom.

55

Frumentus had seen Zenobia standing alone at the cliff top as he led the procession of people into Paradise. He couldn't make out why she was so still, she looked lost in thought, gazing out over the restless world. His instincts told him something was amiss, and once he was certain the folk had safely filed into the garden and onwards towards the doorway he raced over to the still small form of Zenobia. As he reached her he heard her great cry of denial and saw her twisting and leaping two-footed, to fly through the air and over the cliff top.

'Zenobia, don't!' His love for the woman gave him the strength he needed to leap after her flying form and catch hold of her outstretched arms. His body slammed into the hard rock on the top of the cliff. Zenobia crashed into the side of the cliff face. Frumentus had her and he was not letting go. Slowly and painfully he pulled her up over the top of the cliff where the two held each other tightly, sobbing for breath, eventually rising, painfully aware of what might have been.

'Are you all right, Zenobia? The horses came back alone. I wasn't sure what had happened. I got the people here just as fast as I could. You looked like you were in a trance and then you were lashing out at the air. What was it that you were doing? I was so frightened I would lose you right in front of my eyes. I couldn't face that. I love you, Zenobia. Please don't break my heart by leaving me alone, not like that, not in any way, ever!'

Frumentus stared at the delicate creature before him whose aching inner beauty held his heart captive. He stirred as the sound of fighting reached up from the plain below. 'They've all come, Zenobia, no one is left outside Paradise, just you and me. Shall we go in before the fighting reaches here?'

Zenobia and Frumentus broke their embrace and whilst Frumentus turned to go she remained standing, peering out at the world laid before her, the stranger lost to sight. 'Frumentus, it could have been so beautiful, he showed me that. So much has been lost through greed and hatred. I knew there was something better to come so I resisted Satan, the stranger, and he fled from me. Now I have seen Satan fall.'

56

The sound of conflict rose from the plain below as the clashes intensified. Soon the hawks would prevail and inter-ballistic nuclear warheads would be released to fall upon the beauty of the earth. 'Enoch says it will all end in fire and one final conflict before God comes to make all things new. It seems that it must be so, and I am so saddened by our failure to live well together.' Zenobia sighed 'We're just one giant mistake, a gamble taken by God who wanted to bless us with the dignity of free will and this is the choice we have made. I don't want to turn my back on it all, Frumentus, but it's too late to prevent this from happening.'

Leaning wearily upon Frumentus, Zenobia turned away from the world and walked towards the gates of Paradise, the pair entering together. They passed through the beautiful gardens into the temple following the worn pathway of countless souls. As they entered they were met by the three who stood smiling at them.

'Welcome home, good and faithful servants. Join us and be at peace.' Zenobia's heart was simply overwhelmed as she beheld the sight of hundreds of thousands gathered in the place. She saw Hanok smiling at her as he moved forward to embrace Frumentus.

'So glad you kept listening, old boy, I kept trying to steer you onwards, cheering you as you went. Words just pour out of me in this place. I think you could hear me calling sometimes for you, young Frumentus, are rather unique. Few have tasted Paradise and then left to go back into the world. To do so makes you perceptive of the voices that speak from this place. It seems I may have stumbled into this place in my wonderings, my memory of that is not strong but enough to make me thirsty for a longer taste of the life I found here.'

Frumentus grinned as he gripped his friend's arm. 'They listened to Frumentus the Fool in the end, Hanok. The last and the least, the discarded ones in the homes, they listened, and they came. Isn't it wonderful that some were saved!'

'Yes, my boy, it is. Did you ever find that quote from the bible, the one I hid down the side of my chair to keep from young Dan? I had it underlined for you.' Frumentus offered the book to him.

'Sorry, no, Hanok, I didn't get that much further in reading. It's been quite busy recently!'

'Ah well you see, my boy, if you had made the time you might have come across this. "*But God chose the foolish things of the world to shame the wise; God chose the weak things of the world to shame the strong. God chose the lowly things of this world and the despised things—and the things that are not—to nullify the things that are so that no one may boast before him.*" You, Frumentus, you were chosen, you carried good news to the despised and rejected. News of a better way of life is all over the place in this book. You really ought to read it. It has so many great words and to know the meaning of words – the ideas, hopes and dreams that they convey, is an adventure, a treasure to seek!'

57

Zenobia embraced Spiro. 'My friend, you were dead, now you are alive, but more so!'

Picking her up and twirling her around like a child, Spiro grinned. 'Yes, alive and refreshed and awaiting the renewal of all things when we who are gathered will all taste life. Not endless life, not oppressed or restricted life, but life in all its fullness. I can't wait, but we had to, wait, that is. We've been waiting for you to come, to bring them home, to come home yourself, it all depended on you choosing life, rejecting the way of Satan, and you did. Now look, I have people you will want to meet.'

Spiro led Zenobia forward past smiling faces of many people who reached out to her to touch her as she moved through them. Eventual she was brought to a halt at the back of a couple in cheerful conversation. 'Zenobia, here are your parents.'

As the couple turned, Zenobia gasped with shock and delight. The same smiling faces and kind eyes she remembered from her childhood regarded her with calm peace. 'We knew you would come back to us, Zenobia. We prayed so much for you and we trusted you would come through the trials and tests that your hard life has thrown up. It will all be worthwhile, my darling child, you have always been in the mind of your Creator, He loves you as do we. You must go to him. Don't worry, we will always be here waiting for you.'

Zenobia stilled the protesting voice that rose within her at the thought of being sent away again. Reassured that it was to be well, she looked mutely at Spiro. 'It's this way, Frumentus is to come too.'

'What of Dromas, did he come in or was it too late for him?'

'I don't know, Zenobia, I don't see all who come here, but there are some here that surprise me. I know what they were like before, very rough diamonds to say the least! But God looks into the heart and if there is the slightest spark of life He will take that and fan it into a flame of faith. It is only those who stubbornly and continually refuse the offer of life who can't seem to find their way here. Why, I've seen the youngest of children here, surely too young to get here alone. They say they're brought here by their angels and given the chance at life, even if they never had chance to choose it for themselves. It is good here, Zenobia, the place you yearned for all the days of your life.'

Frumentus and Zenobia passed beyond the happy throng into a room where deep baths had been prepared for them. Each sank, unashamedly naked, into the cleansing water where they remained until all traces of grime were gone. Then they rose to don new brilliant white robes, identical to those the great multitude where wearing. They drank deeply from a clear flowing stream and tasted the fruit of the trees that grew on its banks.

Returning to the vast assembly, they saw thrones set up and on the thrones was beauty and majesty whose voice was like the sound of many rivers. He was reading from a tiny scroll. As He read mighty angels blew trumpets whose sound echoed over the face of the earth. The tortured earth split asunder with a violent shaking of the plain below the Great Heights, causing warfare to cease. Those gathered below looked in wonder as the heights themselves began to crumble and fall in monumental engulfing rockslide. The violent shaking continued with the rising dust and debris so vast that the sun was blocked out and darkness descended on the land as if the very heavens themselves had been rolled up like a scroll. Still the trumpets sounded, and the crust of the earth pitched and tossed like a giant awakening from captivity wishing to be free of its chains.

As the rock fell away from the heights the beauty of the Paradise garden and the splendour of the temple was revealed, freed from the concealing rock, a perfect cube dazzling in precious splendour. It hung in the air before graciously and gradually descending towards the plain. Those on the plain fled from its coming, seeking to escape the awesome beauty. As the temple touched the earth a vast sonic wave swept in all directions and everything was caught up in its movement and thrown into the air, a remixing of the fundamental elements of the blue planet was occurring, once again bringing order out of chaos.

As the structure settled, those robed in white emerged from the massive pearly white doors to step onto the plain. What had once been dried and barren now received water that flowed from vast subterranean lakes awakened by the shaking earth to pour forth life-giving water onto the land.

Hanok, Zenobia, Spiro and Frumentus stepped through the doorway. It seemed to them as if the garden of Paradise was simply spreading before their very eyes, life was reaching into the desolate region bringing forth growth. 'This is too wonderful a thing to comprehend, Hanok, what is happening to the land?'

'It's in that book, Frumentus, you really are going to have settle down and read it. We're entering a new age now, I'm not sure if this is eternal life or a one-thousand-year foretaste of it. We've been called forth to share again the work of creation with Him. The whole world is going to be caught up in a renewal of all things and we shall live as we were always intended to. It's an amazing thing, Frumentus, have you looked at yourself, you're not the person you once were. See too Spiro and Zenobia, they are the same yet different. You can recognise them but it's the new physical reality that has caught hold of us all. We'll eat and drink and work and play like before but now the limitations of the old life have finally fallen away, we're reborn as is the creation around us.'

'Hanok, what of the Watchers and the Satan, are they still at large or is evil banished forever?' Zenobia was not anxiously asking the question, it was now as if those times of conflict and pain were becoming untrue. Her question was more of curiosity, she had seen the fall of Satan and the wondered if the Watchers were gone as well.

Hanok drew the three in closer to him. 'We all bear some scars to this day from our struggles with those creatures. Deep below this planet is a molten furnace, it is the eternal home for angels that rebel against God. They cannot die and so their suffering and torment is an awful thing to contemplate; it is endless. I'm sad to say it is also the destination for any humans who refuse the offer to come home. The sad truth is, if they choose to live without God, they will live without God, lost to all good things in a world of darkness and despair. As for us we must learn again what it means to be good stewards of this creation.'

The four friends stood together in quiet wonder at all that they now beheld, excited by the adventure that lay before them; here at last was the end of the beginning. Glorious adventure awaited.

The end